SURGE

Salinity Cove Book One

MAYA NICOLE

D1522770

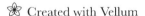 Created with Vellum

Author's Note

Salinity Cove is a reverse harem romance series. That means the main character will have a happily ever after with three or more men.

There is bullying and situations that may make some readers uncomfortable. Recommended for readers 18+ for adult content and language.

This book is dedicated to baby sharks.

Prologue

RILEY

Ten Years Ago

I dug my shovel into the damp sand and scooped it into my bucket. I was a pro at building sandcastles since, nearly every day, my mom brought me to the beach. It was our happy place, and the waves crashing along the shore always made me feel alive.

She'd bring a giant towel to lie on and work on her tan while I perfected my sandcastle sculpting abilities. I might have only been seven, but I was already a master.

After making sure the sand was wet and packed enough, I turned the bucket out onto the damp sand and slid it off the new tower. It was so satisfying sliding the bucket off and seeing the smooth surface ready for me to carve.

"Hon, come here and rub some more lotion on my back." My mom was already tan, but for some reason, always wanted to toast in the sun. "I don't want to burn."

I left my tools and buckets and ran over to her, taking the brown bottle from her outstretched hand. I squirted a glob onto her back and rubbed it into her smooth skin.

My mom was what many called a classic beauty, with the same green eyes as me. She looked younger than she was, and I heard her make comments about being a cougar on a regular basis. Most of the men who walked by her on the beach did a double take as they passed.

"Thanks, sweetie. We'll head home for dinner in about thirty minutes." She folded her arms and rested her head on them.

I ran back to my sandcastle and my stomach grew tight. I had misjudged how far the waves would roll in and now a bucket and shovel were headed out to sea.

I took off after them, a wave receding as I ran

forward. The next wave would bring them closer to me again and I could grab them.

The wave hit me in the legs as I ran and I fell to my knees. I got back up and sloshed through the shin-high water.

I was almost to the bucket when another wave crashed against me and I got a mouthful of salt water. I grabbed the bucket and looked around for the shovel.

It must have sunk to the bottom. I turned and started going back toward the shore, but the sand beneath me felt like it gave way and I was pulled backwards.

Panic welled up inside me and I kicked my legs toward the bottom, trying to find my footing. There was just ocean and the increasing sense of dread. I tried to let out a cry for help and felt myself being pulled under by an invisible force.

I clamped my mouth shut and a few bubbles of air escaped anyway.

No, no, no. This isn't happening!

I let the bucket go and flailed my arms, trying with all my strength to swim back to the surface. Why was the water taking me? Why was no one coming to save me?

I was a decent swimmer for a seven-year-old, but instead of my arms and legs moving like they should have, they felt heavy and disjointed from my body.

I was out of air and knew I was about to drown. I squeezed my eyes shut.

My mom had warned me to stay out of the water without her by my side. It had only been for a second to grab my bucket. A second was all the water needed.

The invisible wave was pulling me out to sea.

My body could no longer hold the air and I exhaled, bubbles flying from my nose and mouth. I opened my eyes, trying to find the surface. My entire body burned like I had just played three hours of soccer in the hot sun, and the water filled my ears with a fuzzy sound.

A flash of blue in my periphery caught my attention, and then something wrapped around my waist. My vision narrowed like I was trying to see through a smaller and smaller hole. Then everything went black.

"THERE SHE IS!" I coughed at the sound of my mom's distraught voice. My side was burning and I cried out, struggling to sit up and move away from the hot metal.

"How'd she manage to get up there?" Men's voices began talking in haste about how I was swept out to sea and was able to climb onto a buoy. They said I was the strongest little girl they'd ever seen.

I wiped at my eyes, which were burning from the dried salt water and cried out for my mom. All around me was water as far as the eye could see. I had just been on the shore building a sandcastle, and now I was in the middle of the ocean.

"Hold on, baby!"

A man in an orange jumpsuit jumped into the ocean and swam toward me. He grabbed onto the side of the buoy with one hand and handed me a life jacket with the other. "Put this on, sweetie. I'm going to get you off this thing."

I did as he asked, my arms feeling like jelly as I lifted them to put on the life jacket. Once it was on, he hooked a rope on the front of it. "You're going to have to scoot to the edge and jump off into my arms."

"I'm scared." My chin trembled as I put my legs over the side. The metal was still hot on my skin and my side burned like I had stepped into a shower that was too hot.

"I know it's scary, but I'm right here, and all the other people on the boat are here to help too. You are such a brave girl."

I took a deep breath and pushed off the side. Like he said he would, he caught me as soon as my body hit the water and immediately swam back toward the boat.

A man and woman dressed in the same orange as the man who had gotten me off the buoy pulled me onto the boat.

The woman handed me to my mom, who wrapped me in her arms. She was sobbing and saying how it was all her fault.

"Ow!" Her arm brushed against my side and it felt like it was on fire.

My mom set me down on a bench and took off the life jacket so they could look at my injury. I hid my face against my mom's arm.

"It's a miracle she was pulled this far out and survived." One of the men opened a bag next to me and wiped something that stung on my wound. "We need to get her to the hospital to have these burns from the metal checked out. I'm going to start an IV to get some fluids in her."

The boat engine revved, and I peeked out from where my face was buried as the boat began pulling away. I couldn't even see the shore from where we were.

"How long was she missing?" The man who had cleaned my burn was wrapping gauze around my torso.

"No more than half an hour." My mom rubbed my back. "Sweetie, do you know what happened?"

I shook my head and shut my eyes. I was exhausted. All I remembered was a flash of blue and arms pulling me.

But that couldn't be right. Could it?

Chapter One

RILEY

"This is Brittany Aspen coming to you live, fifty miles off the Monterey coast, where last night an oil well explosion shook the biggest oil platform in the world. At this hour, we are being told that the explosion cracked the sea floor and engineers are concerned other wells may soon follow. It's unclear at this hour if oil has spilled into the Pacific. We will keep you updated as this story unfolds."

Silent observers.

We were the ones that sat back, soaked in the information, and stayed out of trouble and drama.

I'd always been an observer in school and in life.

Quietly doing my job of being an honor student and staying out of the way of those that make school hell. It was enough of a task to keep up with the ins and outs of social hierarchy, without being stuck in the middle of juicy gossip.

It wasn't worth the time and effort to stay on a gilded pedestal when high school was such a short blip in the grand scheme of things. Four years came and four years went. If I lived to be one-hundred, it was merely four percent of my time on Earth.

Yet somehow, a simple book documenting the high school experience had almost a hundred-percent buy rate and took permanent residence on shelves. There was something powerful about producing a yearbook that would be looked at for decades.

"What are you looking at?" I was snapped out of my thoughts by a voice dripping in honey. There was a flutter in my stomach and my neck heated.

I knew exactly who it was without even looking up. But I wanted to look up because Jax West was the most attractive man at Salinity Cove High School. He was definitely a man and not a boy.

My eyes traveled up his long, muscular legs to his narrow waist and broad shoulders. I squinted and shielded my eyes to get a better view of his face.

I was all too familiar with Jax, but so was every other girl at school. Most of us drooled over him at a distance. He was one of the elite swimmers at school and was the captain of the swim team. With that came a chip on his shoulder that translated into broken hearts and midnight tears.

I had to admit, his asshole tendencies were muted by the angle of his jaw and hypnotic aqua eyes. He was hot, and he was talking to me for the first time. Now I understood how so many fell under his spell.

"Excuse me?" I fumbled with the brochures in my lap and squinted at him again. I was nothing if not smooth while talking to guys.

He sat down next to me, a smile playing on his lips. I opened my mouth to ask him why he was here in the first place, but closed it.

Don't make a fool of yourself, Riley.

He grabbed the top booklet. "Stanford?"

His proximity got the best of me, despite my best efforts. "What are you even doing here?" I snatched it back from him and he frowned, causing my stomach to twist. "Is there a swim camp going on?"

"I needed another elective, and last night, Mr. Garcia emailed me and invited me to this little planning sesh you had going."

Jax was going to be on the yearbook staff? He had to be kidding. I doubted he had the time to dedicate to creating a book people would look back on in twenty years and show their kids.

"You? On yearbook?" I was setting a really good first impression. "It takes a lot of time and commitment to publish. Usually only spring sport athletes can handle the time commitment."

"I need the elective. Mr. Garcia thinks it will be good to have an athlete of my caliber lend their expertise to the sports section." He took the rest of my college brochures and flipped through them. "Aren't you going to your father's alma mater?"

I had been worried all summer about my classmates knowing Robert Kline was my father. My fears had just been confirmed.

I looked across the quad and frowned. I should have been enjoying myself on the beautiful Santa Cruz campus, but instead, my mind kept wandering to the headlines over the past several weeks.

250 million gallons of oil spill into the Pacific.
Marine life at risk.
Robert Kline in hiding.

My father was a sore subject that I didn't want to talk about. I didn't even know the man, but the thought of being related to him made me want to vomit. He was a coward and a criminal who ran instead of dealing with the aftermath of what was being called the greatest oil disaster *ever*.

"I want to keep my options open." Our fingers touched as he held out the brochures. My fingers tingled, and he propped his leg up, draping an arm over it and staring at me.

I shifted on the grass and shoved the college brochures into my messenger bag. I'd gathered them at the beginning of summer when my best friends and I went on a road trip to visit campuses.

"Your skin reminds me of the sands of Waimanalo Bay." It was an odd thing for him to compare my skin to, but maybe this was why he had girls hanging all over him.

"Is that supposed to be a compliment?" I put the strap of my bag over my head and shoulders.

He laughed. "It's a compliment. Have you been? It's in Hawaii." He reached out and grabbed a lock of my wavy brown hair that was tied up in a ponytail, rubbing it between his fingers as I shook my head. "Let's hang out."

My eyes widened and my heart nearly beat out of my chest. "What? Hang out?"

I wanted to run away and hide my face somewhere. This entire interaction with him was messing with my head. Heat spread across my neck and up to my cheeks.

Was he really asking me out on a date? *The* Jax West, king of the school, was asking me, Riley Kline, to go out with him?

I was nothing compared to the girls who hung off him on a daily basis. He went through them like a baby goes through diapers. They were the girls who spent two hours in the morning doing their hair and make-up. I was the girl that didn't even spend a quarter of that on special occasions, much less for going to school.

He looked at his phone. "Yeah, it'll be fun. What else do you have to do?"

"Why?" I was so confused because the Tritons, as they liked to call themselves, didn't hang out with the lower echelon of the high school hierarchy.

He threw his head back and laughed, giving me a great view of his Adam's apple and his smile. "Can't a guy just want to hang out?" His aqua eyes darkened as they met mine and my heart skipped a beat.

He stood and held out his hand. I looked up at him and hesitated. Guys like Jax didn't give me the time of day. I was considered a bookworm, and our crowds rarely crossed paths.

I took his hand, and he pulled me to my feet before he reached out and grabbed the strap of my bag that had slipped down my arm. His knuckles brushed across my bare skin and my nipples tingled in response.

My traitorous body needed to chill out. I didn't have time to let my hormones run amuck when college applications were right around the corner. All it took was one bad choice to have everything I had worked for come crumbling down.

I needed to text Ivy immediately to get her take on this whole situation. Sure, I had crushes, but I had never hung out with a guy alone before. It wasn't for a lack of them trying. I just had no interest.

I *should* make more of an effort for senior year. I wanted to have all the typical high school experiences; homecoming, prom, senior activities. Most of my important classes for college were complete, but could I afford the distractions a boyfriend or dating brought?

And did I want to draw the attention of the likes of Jax West?

He walked next to me toward the building where the yearbook planning sessions were taking place. Every year, yearbook staffs were invited to a summer weekend of workshops and planning. It was a great way to get a head start on the book.

"I was thinking we could order a pizza and watch a movie." Jax put his arm around my shoulder and I stiffened. "Relax, it's just an arm."

Just an arm.

Something told me it wasn't just an arm, but maybe hanging out with Jax would be a good thing to help me come out of my shell. My mom might even get off my back about being more social outside of my tight-knit group of friends.

AFTER CONVINCING Jax that it would be better to eat pizza with the rest of the yearbook staff who had attended, he took my hand and we walked down the path toward the dorms. The sun was setting, and I felt out of place walking hand-in-hand with him.

I didn't understand what he saw in me. There

was a cheerleading camp going on too; he could have easily had any of those girls.

He stopped at a fountain and sat down, pulling me down next to him. "Am I making you uncomfortable?" He squeezed my hand and looked at me with his hypnotizing eyes.

"You aren't making me uncomfortable. I'm confused though." I crossed my leg and then uncrossed it.

"Confused?" He scooted closer so that the sides of our thighs touched. The fabric of his board shorts slid across the bare skin of my leg. "What is there to be confused about?"

I held up our clasped hands and then let go, bringing my hands together in my lap. "There are thousands of girls on this campus right now, and probably a frat party or two you could get in to."

He leaned forward with his forearms on his knees and looked over at me. "Why is it hard to believe I'd find you attractive? There might be a thousand girls within swiping distance, but that doesn't mean that's what I'm in the mood for." I scrunched my nose, and he flinched before laughing and standing. "That came out wrong."

"I'm not interested in being someone's mood for the evening." I stood and started to walk away.

He jogged to catch up and blocked my path. "Just come watch a movie with me. What else are you going to do?"

"Read." After I binge watched the most recent season of *Riverdale* with a bottle of Sprite and a shareable-size bag of Skittles.

"Come on, you can't be serious. One movie and then you'll still have time to read before bed." He smiled and shoved his hands in his pockets. "I promise, no funny business."

I looked around as if someone was going to jump out and save me from the awkwardness I felt. "Fine." I rolled my eyes when he did a fist pump in the air.

I couldn't believe I'd given in and gone back to his dorm room with him to watch a movie. I knew deep down inside that this was probably a ploy to try to get in my pants, but he had been too charismatic.

"Can you see okay?" He had put his laptop on a chair next to the bed.

I nodded and sat back against the pillow I'd placed against the wall. My stomach was filled with butterflies as he sat next to me after pressing play. His arm brushed against mine and he looked over at me and smiled.

About twenty minutes into the action movie, he put his hand on my thigh. I kept my eyes locked on his computer screen and willed myself to stay calm. I didn't *hate* the way his warm hand felt against my bare skin.

What would it be like to kiss him? His thumb moved across my skin in a sweeping motion. My body tingled at his touch and trying to focus on the movie was no longer an option.

I braved a glance over at him and met his stare. His eyes darkened and they moved down to my lips. Holy shit, was he going to kiss me?

I licked my lips in anticipation. I'd only kissed a boy once and it was in sixth grade, during science camp. I inwardly cursed that I was about to kiss a seasoned pro when I had only kissed a prepubescent boy and my hand.

Before I could even process that it was actually happening, he leaned in and his lips brushed mine. I turned my body toward him, causing his hand to move to my inner thigh, right at the hem of my shorts.

If my body was on fire from just a simple kiss and touch, I didn't even want to imagine what taking it further would feel like, but my mind went there anyway.

His lips moved against mine gently, and I tentatively moved mine. I was trembling and hoped I wasn't a bad kisser.

He brought his other hand to my hair and gripped the back of my head, pulling me closer and deepening the kiss. I whimpered as his tongue slid between my lips and found my tongue.

Now I understood why people made out all the time. It was causing my body to burn with desire and a tingling sensation to build in my core. I was no stranger to feeling horny, but this was different. I could almost feel what it would be like to have his hands glide across where only mine had been.

I couldn't let it get that far though. I knew him, but it wasn't like we'd even said two words to each other before today.

The hand on my thigh moved to the button on my shorts and I pushed his chest to break the kiss. "What are you doing?"

His hand stilled on the button, and his other hand moved out of my hair to caress my cheek. "I want to make you feel good."

My breaths were quick and unsteady as he licked his lips and looked down to where his hand lay against the button. One of his knuckles brushed the skin right above it, and it almost made me give in to my desires. Would it be so bad if I let him?

I scooted off the bed and stood in the center of the room. "I should go." I adjusted my top and shorts as I put on my sandals.

"Did I do something wrong?" He closed his laptop screen and stretched his arms over his head as he stood. My eyes were instantly drawn to his shirt riding up to show his toned lower abdomen with the delicious V that led into his shorts.

"No." I wasn't about to tell him he was my first meaningful kiss and I really did want to let him unbutton my shorts and do magical things with his fingers. "We have an early start tomorrow and I'm tired."

He grabbed his phone and typed something before sliding it into his back pocket. "I'll walk you back to your dorm building then." He grabbed his keys and followed me out of his room and into the cool night.

I wrapped my arms around myself as we walked down the path to the dorm building that was for girls only. He followed me inside, and I stopped to face him.

"I don't think you're supposed to be in here." I looked around, but the building was quiet besides the faint sounds of televisions coming through the thin doors.

"It'll be fine. The adults are probably off drinking." He brushed past me and went up the stairs.

We got to my room and I unlocked the door. "Well, thanks."

I knew as soon as I opened the door a crack that something was wrong inside. The smell that hit me made my stomach curdle, and I put my hand over my mouth as I flicked on the light.

"What the hell?" Jax put his hands on my arms as I backed up into him. "Who would do something like this?"

He moved me to the side and walked into the room. I gagged and brought the hem of my shirt up to cover my mouth and nose.

There were dead fish covered in oil everywhere. They were covering the bed and in my suitcase, which had been shut. I choked on a sob and Jax grabbed a folded white piece of paper from the desk.

"Ms. Kline, you've been canceled." His mouth was set in a tight line and he threw the note onto the bed. "Sounds like a threat. Why would someone do this?"

Tears filled my eyes and I backed all the way

into the hall and against the opposite door. "I don't know." My voice was muffled from the shirt and my tears.

He stalked toward me and stopped abruptly, his eyes falling to my left side. I quickly let go of my shirt and pulled it down to cover the faint silvery flesh of my burn scar. It wasn't bad, but it was noticeable.

"What happened?"

"Burned it on a buoy." It sounded ridiculous, but I didn't need to relive the trauma from that day by explaining further. The burn hadn't been as bad as it could have been.

He looked slightly taken aback, and then he stepped forward and took my face in his hands. I tried to ignore the fact that they had oil on them from him picking up the note. "Why would someone threaten you? You have to have some idea. Dead fish and oil? That's specific."

The tears were falling freely now, and he swiped them with his oily thumbs. "My father, but I-"

"You need to call and tell him. The fish and the note are definitely a threat. He should come pick you up." His posture was stiff and he sounded angry. If anyone should have been angry about the fish, it should be me.

Instead, I was numb.

"What's going on here?" A female teacher rounded the corner of the hall and glanced into my room. "What in the world?"

Jax stepped away from me, his beautiful features marred with a sneer. He was looking at me as if he were disgusted with me, but it was probably from the smell emanating from the dorm room.

I swallowed the lump in my throat. "Someone broke in."

"Jesus. Let's call your advisor and get you to a new room." She wrapped an arm around my shoulders and looked at Jax. "And you need to leave."

Jax walked ahead of us to the stairs and glanced at me over his shoulder. His eyes flashed with an emotion I couldn't pinpoint, and then he was down the stairs without a word.

Chapter Two

"*T*his year is going to be the best year ever!" My best friend, Ivy, slid into the passenger seat of my car, her long red hair nearly smacking me in the face as she whipped her head around to grab the seatbelt. "My goal this year is to be more organized, so let's hit up school supplies first before we go to the mall."

I laughed and pulled away from the curb. Ivy and I had been friends since elementary school, when we discovered our shared love for the Jonas Brothers. We both decided early on to stay out of drama at school, especially when everyone was team Nick or team Joe and we were the only ones that were team Kevin.

It had been three weeks since the fish incident

and school would start the following week. I was normally excited for school, but my stomach had been in knots wondering what would be in store for me. I was foolish to think that no one would connect me to my father. My last name was, unfortunately, Kline and he was from Salinity Cove himself.

Jax hadn't responded to the texts I sent him asking him if he wanted to hang out. I guess the fish had been a wake-up call that I was not the girl for him. Or he had just been lonely and I'd been convenient.

"Are you doing okay?" Ivy turned down the volume of the music and watched me as I drove onto the highway. "You have circles under your eyes."

"I haven't been sleeping well." I glanced over at her to see concern written on her face. "What if-"

"Don't start that again. It was probably some idiot who thought he was being funny. Nothing else has happened, has it?" She put her hand on my forearm and gave it a gentle squeeze.

The police had been called but wrote the incident off as a stupid high school prank by bored teenagers. I wanted to believe that was the case, but deep down I knew it was because of my father.

I shook my head and focused on the road. I didn't want to talk about my father or the ongoing aftermath of his oil company. It was all over the news on a daily basis. I had nothing to do with his oil business, yet I was starting to feel guilt over it.

I never advertised who my father was, but somehow, people in Salinity Cove still knew. He was born and raised here before moving away to attend business school and eventually became the largest offshore oil tycoon in the world after taking over his family's oil company.

The fish had been a reminder that I *was* a Kline despite him leaving my mom before I could crawl. My mom did get money from him, but that was as far as our relationship went.

"Jax hasn't texted me back. I've decided that it was a fluke and he must have been high." I twisted my lips to the side. "Maybe it's the wrong number."

He had texted himself from my phone, but the possibility was still there. That made me feel a little better, but not by much. He had left camp the next morning. Mr. Garcia said something about him being double booked.

"Forget about him. You don't want a guy like him, Ri. He'll use you then leave you crying just like every other girl." She sighed. "I wish they all weren't so pretty to look at though."

I pulled off the highway and parked. This shopping trip was just what I needed. I lived for school supplies and would rather spend more on amazing pens and sticky notes than clothes.

We headed down each aisle, taking our time deciding what binders and other essentials we needed. I loved being organized for school, and I couldn't keep the smile off my face.

"Excuse me." I was squatting down when the thick, velvety voice interrupted my contemplation between a white binder and a blue one.

I stood and nearly bumped heads with Blake Huron. I stepped back and winced. Of all people to bump into on an outing that was supposed to be distracting me, a Triton was the last person I wanted to bump into.

Blake was the quietest of the three. He smiled down at me and I was nearly knocked back from how bright and welcoming it was. He might have been the quietest, but in a way he was the loudest.

He rubbed his jaw and laughed softly. "Riley Kline." I didn't know why he was telling me my name, I knew who I was.

With as rich as his family was, I was surprised he wasn't ordering diamond encrusted binders.

"Hi." I lifted my hand in a wave and immediately wanted to crawl into a hole and have staples shot at me. Hi? I couldn't do any better than *hi*?

Blake was just as skilled at swimming as Jax and was the envy of most males at Salinity Cove High. Swimming ranked above even football, which was saying a lot considering we had a championship winning team.

His eyes gave me a once over before he bent down and pulled a blue binder off the shelf. "Well, see you in a few days."

My mouth parted as he walked away without looking back. I'd definitely be seeing him since the Tritons attracted the eyes of most females, including me.

"Did Blake Huron just check you out?" Ivy grabbed my arm as she squealed a little. "Girl, two of them have now talked to you!"

"I'm not sure that's necessarily a good thing, Ivy." I grabbed the same binder as Blake and threw it in my cart that was already overloaded with more than I needed. "Let's go. More stores await."

We headed to the checkout just as Blake exited

the store. I blew out a breath, stirring the hair framing my face.

"This card is declined." The cashier handed me back my credit card. "Do you have cash or another card?"

"That's not possible." I handed her a second card and she swiped it. I was certain I had money on the cards. My mom topped them off monthly, not that I spent a whole lot anyway.

"Declined."

My stomach dropped and Ivy stepped beside me, holding out her card. "Try this one."

Her card went through, and I took my bags as she rang up Ivy's assortment of school supplies. While I was waiting, I sent a text to my mom, hoping she'd respond.

She had left a week ago needing to *get away from it all.* I understood, and I would have gone with her if school hadn't been about to start. I was almost eighteen and was more than ready to be left on my own for a few weeks.

"You should call the number on the back of the card." Ivy looped her arm through mine and we headed to the car. "That happened to me once when my dad forgot to pay my bill."

I called the number once we got to the car. After

waiting several minutes, an account representative came on the phone. "Both cards are empty."

"That's impossible. I haven't used them for anything except gas." I frowned. "What are the charges? Maybe someone stole the numbers."

"It looks like a week ago they were cashed out by the main account holder."

My stomach dropped. "That's not me." My mom was the main account holder. Why would she take all the money she put on the cards?

"Have you spoken to the other person on the account, a Natalia Hernandez Moreno?"

After getting off the phone with the credit card company, I called my mom's cell and it went straight to voicemail. She hadn't replied to my text either. If she was lying on the beach in the Maldives, she probably didn't even have her phone with her.

"When was the last time you talked to your mom?" Ivy looked concerned, but it wasn't like she hadn't left me alone for a weekend here and there in the past year or two.

"She texted me when she got to the airport, but that's been it." Unless there was an emergency, she said she wouldn't text me until she got back.

"I can buy whatever you need and you can pay

me back later." Ivy's lips twisted to the side. I hoped it was just a fluke.

I COULDN'T BELIEVE it was the first day of senior year. I was still unable to get ahold of my mom, but it had only been a few days, and luckily, I had a great friend that fronted me the money for clothes and a few other essentials.

I parked my car next to Ivy's and grabbed my bag from the passenger seat. The senior section of the lot was already half-full of excited students greeting each other with hugs and handshakes. We'd made it.

The senior parking lot was where a lot of drama occurred, and it made my stomach tighten as I slid out and shut my door. Last year there had been so many incidents that they had installed security cameras over the break.

"Ri!" Ivy pulled me into a hug and passed me off to Aiden, who lifted me off the ground in a bear hug.

Aiden was another close friend, except he didn't stay out of the limelight as much as Ivy and I did.

He strutted the halls as if he was on the hunt at all times.

"Girl. That hair." He clucked his tongue and flicked my ponytail. I hadn't gone to get it cut and refused to let Ivy pay for something that could be fixed with a hair tie. "How are we supposed to catch you a man if you wear your hair pulled back like that? You need to let them see what they can run their hands through."

"A real man will see her ponytail as an opportunity." Ivy wiggled her eyebrows suggestively.

I rolled my eyes. "I don't need a man. Especially one that likes to pull hair." The idea of a man pulling my hair as he did unthinkable things did make me curious. "They cause nothing but trouble."

I walked with them toward the gates leading into school and spotted the Tritons and their crew near the entrance.

"Is that why you sucked face with-" Ivy smacked Aiden in the arm and he clamped his mouth shut. "I mean, you're right, Riley. Men are nothing but trouble." He laughed. "Trouble I wouldn't mind getting involved in, if you know what I'm saying."

As we passed the group gathered near the gates, I kept my eyes in front of me. It was mortifying to make out with a guy and have him ghost you. Had I been that bad?

"You know what I heard? Her pussy reeks of dead fish." I glanced in the direction of the nasally voice and almost stumbled over my feet.

The group of four girls was staring right at me. They were the popular girls, and not the ones that were nice. They were the ones that used every opportunity to remind others that they were nothing more than a waste of space. I was glad none of them were ever in my classes.

I increased my pace through the outdoor halls toward the corridor of lockers mine was in. Ivy split from us with a quick wave, and Aiden leaned against the locker next to mine as I unloaded supplies.

I hoped that it had just been a coincidence they were talking about dead fish and looking at me. Who was I kidding? They were, and now it was going to bother me the rest of the day.

I headed toward homeroom with Aiden. Most of our classes were the same, with a few exceptions.

"Stop worrying. We've got your back." Aiden looped his arm through mine and we walked into Advanced English.

We were a few of the first to class, so we chose

seats in the back. I might have been a top student, but I liked seeing the entire room.

I was getting my notebook and pen out when I heard Aiden gasp, and I turned my head toward him. "What?"

"Blake Huron just walked in and is headed straight for the seat next to you," he said under his breath.

Blake had never been in any of our classes. It wasn't that he wasn't capable of handling honors and AP classes, but he was rumored to pay other students to do his work for him.

I sat back in my chair and our eyes met as he walked down the row. He had a cocky grin on his face and his dark brown eyes sparkled. Out of the three Tritons, he was the most approachable.

He dropped the blue binder he had picked out at the office supply store on the desk and slid into the seat next to me. He moved it over so his knee touched mine. I scrunched my nose and moved my desk an inch.

He laughed. "Imagine my surprise seeing we have English together." He angled his body toward mine and I sat up straighter. I didn't know what the hell was going on.

If my stomach kept seizing up like it was, I was

going to end up with an ulcer. Why were they all of a sudden taking interest in me? It couldn't be a coincidence that first Jax had approached me and now Blake.

Was it because of my father? Were they curious to get firsthand information from his daughter? They had to know I had nothing to do with him.

"Back off, Huron." Aiden leaned forward and pinned him with a glare. "Our kind don't put up with your bullshit in our classes."

"*Your* kind?" He flinched. "*You* of all people should know the harm of those words."

Aiden flinched. "I didn't mean it like that. I meant in advanced classes we are focused and drama free."

Blake moved his desk a few inches from mine. "We'll see about that. It seems you don't know your classmates very well."

Class started, and all I felt was Blake's eyes burning into the side of my head. I tried to concentrate on the expectations for the semester, but it was nearly impossible with his proximity and gaze.

Why wasn't the teacher asking him to move his desk back to the row?

"Since this is your senior year and most of you will be attending college next fall, we will start to focus on some of the skills you will need to success-fully make the transition. Starting with a study group." I was a few sentences behind processing what she was saying. "You will be placed in small groups and meet two times a month to work on your assignments and get support from each other."

I internally groaned. I didn't mind group work with certain people, but even in advanced classes there were a few that just coasted along not caring about their grades. They made more work for the rest of us.

"I know you might not feel like you need it, but next year, you might find you need to work with others to continue your success. It's a whole other world filled with distractions, and a study group will help you stay on track." She then pointed around to make groups of four.

"Did you hear that, Kline?" A shiver ran down my spine as Blake leaned over and whispered in my ear. "We're going to be *study* buddies."

"Mr. Huron." Mrs. Williams' voice held a warn-ing. "Is there something you'd like to share with the class?"

I did an inner squeal of delight at him being called out for talking. I was a senior, but there was still joy to be had over the class disruption getting put in their place.

"Mrs. Williams, I was answering Riley's question."

No. Hell no, he wasn't about to make up something to get me in trouble. What grade were we in?

"And what is that?" She crossed her arms over her chest and looked between me and Blake. Mrs. Williams might have been a newer teacher on the staff, but she was one of the best.

"I can't repeat it. It was grossly inappropriate, and probably sexual harassment." He sounded so sincere that even I believed I had been inappropriate.

A few students in the class giggled, and Mrs. Williams narrowed her eyes at Blake. "And you expect me to believe that?"

I had never had Mrs. Williams as a teacher before, but I assumed most teachers had knowledge of the top students.

Disruptions in advanced classes weren't tolerated.

"Ma'am, if I told my father what you allowed to go on in your classroom, he would not be happy." Everyone knew that Blake's father, as well as Jax's father, had major pull in the town of Salinity Cove.

Their families had been here since it became a town.

Her hands fell to her sides and she cleared her throat. "Ms. Kline, if you and Blake are done being inappropriate, I'll get on with my lesson for the day."

I nodded, and Blake sat back in his chair with a smirk. Whatever the hell he was up to, I didn't like it one bit.

Chapter Three

RILEY

*B*lake was in three out of the four classes I had before lunch. I breathed a sigh of relief during fourth period. He sat next to me in each class and distracted me to the point where I missed half of what the teachers had said.

Lunch rolled around, and I wished we were still allowed off campus as seniors. A few idiots had to ruin it for all of us. I liked lunch, but knowing the three of *them* would be there made me lose my appetite.

I had yet to run into Morgan, the third member of their tight-knit crew, but sensed it was only a matter of time. He was just as attractive as Blake and Jax, but had the bad boy persona down solid. He had a motorcycle that looked like it would be better suited for a raceway instead of the streets of Salinity Cove.

"Girl." Aiden grabbed my arm and steered me away from the cafeteria as I walked across the quad area. "We can't go in there." He led me in the opposite direction toward the parking lot. "Ivy is going to bring us lunch in my car."

My footsteps faltered before I sped up to keep up with his long strides. "Why? What's going on?"

"I heard the Tritons are paying Melissa to jump you in the cafeteria." He unlocked his car and opened the back door for me. "We can hide you better in the back."

I was grateful the gates to the parking lot hadn't been locked and security hadn't stopped us. My chest felt like someone had plopped down on it and I did as he directed. I had never been in any type of altercation. I wouldn't even know how to defend myself if someone started a fight.

"Maybe you should try calling your mom again and see if she'll call you out of school." Aiden turned in his seat and he reached back to squeeze my knee. "Those fuckers can't do this to you."

"I don't understand why they're doing this." I got my phone out of my backpack and tried my mom again. "It still goes straight to voicemail."

I was starting to grow increasingly worried that she wasn't calling me back. I Googled the hotel she told me she was staying at and dialed. It would be past midnight there, but I was desperate.

A heavily accented voice picked up the phone. Sweat beaded on the small of my back.

"Hello. I'm Riley Kline. I'm trying to get ahold of my mother, Natalia Hernandez Moreno. She should have checked in a few days ago."

"Just a moment." I heard the man typing and then he made a clucking noise. "Spell that." I spelled her name. "There's no one here with that name."

"Can you check again?" I watched out the front window as Ivy approached carrying an armful of wrapped sandwiches, drinks, and chips. My stomach rolled with nausea.

"No. Are you sure it's this hotel? There is one other hotel on this island, or you could have the wrong island."

I hung up and tried the second hotel. I got the same response. There were a lot of islands in the Maldives. Maybe I had gotten the wrong one. A few started with the same syllable.

I pulled up a list of islands and my heart sank. It

would take me days to call all the resorts across the islands.

"Is it possible she lied about where she was going? Maybe she's having a sordid affair with a billionaire that owns his own island?" Aiden was trying to make me feel better, but it didn't help.

My mom was missing.

Ivy climbed into the car and Aiden put on music as she passed out food. We were quiet for several minutes as we dug into our sandwiches. I couldn't pass up a turkey sandwich, despite feeling sick.

"Oh, shit." Aiden said with a mouthful of chips. "Duck down and pull that blanket over you."

I followed the direction of his stare and cursed. Melissa was headed straight toward the car, fists clenched at her sides.

Melissa was one of those girls who didn't require a last name to know which Melissa people were talking about. She was one of the toughest girls in the school, and it was rumored she liked to fight in illegal fights.

I climbed onto the floorboard and pulled the blanket over me. It smelled gross and I gagged thinking about what Aiden used it for.

There was a knock on Ivy's window and I heard the window roll down a bit. "Can I help you?"

"Where is she?" I held my breath at the sound of Melissa's rough voice. It came from smoking like a chimney and probably too many dicks shoved down her throat.

"Who?" Aiden popped another chip in his mouth and chewed.

"You know who." I heard her try the back door and then slam her hand against the window. I was glad his back windows were heavily tinted. "I know she's back there."

"Do we need to call security?" Ivy's voice sounded calm, but I could tell she was nervous by the slight unsteadiness. "We don't know who you're looking for."

"Bullshit. You bought three of everything. I watched you."

"You must be seeing things." Aiden laughed. "Time to visit the school nurse to get those peepers checked."

I tried not to laugh at the tone of his voice. Despite my face being threatened by her fists, he was having fun goading her.

"Listen." Her voice dropped to a whisper. "They are out for her blood and I need the money."

I heard Ivy unzip her bag. "How much are they paying you?"

Ivy couldn't seriously be thinking about paying her off. That would work for the time being, but the Tritons were loaded and could pay her even more.

My calf was starting to cramp from being bent at an odd angle. They needed to get rid of her before I made a sound.

"Five."

"Hundred?" Aiden screeched. "You would sell your soul for five hundred dollars?"

"Yeah, well, desperate times. Not all of us have mommies and daddies that take care of us." Melissa's parents had plenty of money. What she really meant to say was that she needed it for drugs.

"Here. Now leave." Ivy huffed, and I heard the window roll back up. "It's clear now."

It might have been clear from Melissa, but it was far from over.

———————

SEVENTH PERIOD WAS my favorite time of day; yearbook. I loved creating art through pictures and capturing special moments that people would cherish.

I sat at my usual computer station and started chatting with Tory, who had been in yearbook with me since freshman year, when Jax yanked open the door ceremoniously and prowled into the room with me set in his sights.

My words stuttered out of my mouth as his eyes locked on mine. His jaw was set, and he looked like he was thinking of all the ways he could hurt me. He had been nice only weeks before and had done a complete one-eighty. It was like he was a different person.

"What the fuck?" Tory whispered as he came to stand behind her.

"Move." His voice was low and held a threat.

I was done with whatever they were up to. I had hidden out during lunch and then avoided them during sixth period. There wasn't anything he could do in the yearbook lab. I did wish Mr. Garcia would hurry up though, but he was still in the room where he taught sophomore English.

"Excuse me?" Tory spun in her chair and glared up at him. "These are editor seats. Go sit in one of the seats up there." She gestured to the other three rows of computers in front of us.

He leaned forward and braced his hands on the

computer desk on either side of her. "This is my seat now. Move, or I'll make you."

"What the hell is wrong with you? You can't just waltz in here like you own the place." I met his eyes as he turned his head and glared at me. "You can go sit and spin."

How could he go from kissing me so gently and caressing my thigh to paying someone to beat my ass? I wasn't one for confrontation, but sitting by quietly wasn't an option.

"Riley, what's going on here? We don't speak to new staff members that way when we can hardly get a full staff as it is." Mr. Garcia entered the room and glanced at us briefly before sitting at his computer and pressing a button to display his computer screen. "Mr. West. Find a seat in the first three rows. You have to earn the right to sit back there."

Mr. Garcia for the win. I smiled sweetly at Jax, and he shoved off the desk, causing the monitor to shake violently. Tory glared daggers at him as he walked to a computer directly in front of us.

She mouthed, "What the fuck?" to me and turned forward as Mr. Garcia started going over expectations and grading.

I hoped Jax wasn't serious about being on yearbook because that would mean I'd have to spend even more time around him outside of the normal school day.

"We've got some new folks on staff this year. Yearbook is going to become your second home, and when it comes close to deadlines, it *will* be your second home." Mr. Garcia displayed a list of stay late days where we would work on finishing layouts for proofing outside of seventh period. "Same as last year, Ashley will be collecting forty dollars from everyone to order dinners throughout the semester."

I stared at the back of Jax, wondering if he'd even be able to stay late with his intense swimming schedule. The swim team at Salinity Cove was the top in the entire state of California, if not the country.

And it was all thanks to *them*. They were the school's elite swimmers that were more than likely headed for the Olympics and countless national and world titles.

"Is that okay with you, Riley?" Mr. Garcia interrupted my thoughts and I jumped slightly.

"Sorry. What?"

He gave me a concerned look and gestured at

the screen. "You'll be in charge of the sports section since you take such fantastic action photos."

I frowned. I did enjoy taking pictures of sports, but I thought we had discussed me being copy editor. "If that's what you want me to do."

I skimmed through the list of names and slumped in the chair, shaking my head. Tory must have sensed my panic because she put her hand on my arm.

Jax West would be on the sports staff. It only made sense, and he had said as much weeks ago. Still, seeing it with my own eyes made it become reality.

"The last ten minutes, I'd like for you to share with your new teams what you did over the summer." Everyone groaned and Mr. Garcia laughed. He just liked to torture us.

We rearranged ourselves into our teams, and Jax sat right next to me. I didn't have to look at him to feel his presence. With our seats in a tight circle, his shoulder nearly bumped mine with how wide they were.

I had seen him in photos without a shirt on, and he wore the swimmer's body better than anyone I had ever seen, including Olympic athletes. He had a long torso with broad, muscular shoulders and abs that were enough to get me to get back in the water.

"All right, I'll start." I moved my chair a smidgen away from Jax. "Besides the yearbook retreat, I visited ten colleges, got some reading done, and completed a level in my dance program."

"Are we allowed to ask questions?" Jax turned his body toward me so the distance I had created disappeared.

His leg touched mine, and all I could focus on was the heat permeating through my jeans. He cleared his throat after a moment and I blinked at him. "Questions?"

"Yeah, about what you did over the summer." He smirked. "Your answers aren't satisfying my curiosity."

"Is there something going on between you two?" Ashley asked with a roll of the eyes.

"No." We both answered at the same time, and the others laughed.

The last thing I wanted was for people to get the impression that something was going on with me and Jax. He was hot, but that didn't detract from the fact that he and his friends were taking a not so positive interest in me.

"Ask whatever questions you want."

"Are we talking ballet or exotic dancing?" The group laughed.

My ears felt like they were burning and I scrunched my nose. "Not that I have anything against exotic dancers, they can make a lot of money and express themselves in a way a lot of us can't, but no. I ballroom dance. I've been doing it since freshman year."

"Isn't that for old people?" Ashley was getting on my nerves. She was usually not a problem, but maybe Jax's attitude was influencing her.

"No. There are plenty of younger people who ballroom dance." Yes, I was one of the few dance students still in high school, but didn't any of them watch *Dancing With the Stars* or *So You Think You Can Dance*? "Who's next?"

"What kind of books do you read?" Ashton asked.

I didn't know how to answer that. I read a lot instead of watching television or playing video games and had discovered a whole new world through indie authors. I decided to keep it vague. "Paranormal stuff."

Ashley laughed and my face heated. She knew what I read because I had recommended several books to her last year. "Don't be shy. We're supposed to get to know one and other better. She reads reverse harem."

"Harem as in multiple partners?" Ashton's mouth hung open. "That's-"

I rolled my eyes. "The woman has three or more love interests and doesn't choose. They all love her and protect her. It's empowering to read." Jax's stare made me shift in my seat. "Jax, what did you do over the summer?"

"Swimming." We all looked at him to continue as he stared back at me. "I also volunteered my time with a non-profit organization that rehabilitates marine life affected by human negligence."

So much loathing dripped from his voice that we all reared back. He said human like he wanted to murder everyone in their sleep.

The rest of the group quickly shared before class ended. Once the bell rang, I pretended to be working on the computer until Jax left. I'd had enough confrontation for one day.

"Riley, make sure you shut the door all the way when you leave. I have a meeting." Mr. Garcia clicked off the projector and walked through the inner door that connected the classrooms in the building.

Jax walked out of the room without a glance back, and I breathed a sigh of relief. "Thank fuck."

Tory laughed. "He is something else. I guess when you have a body like that there has to be some kind of flaw to make the universe happy." She picked up her bag and turned off her screen. "See you tomorrow."

I was left alone and shut down my computer before taking a minute to put my head in my hands. Senior year was supposed to be the best year of high school. We were entering adulthood and making decisions that would affect our futures. We weren't supposed to act like children. Targeting me for something my father's company did was ridiculous.

"Riley." My head snapped up and I was face to face with Jax, who had somehow snuck back in the room without a sound. He was leaning against the door.

I put my bag over my shoulder and stood. "Stay away from me."

He laughed and held up his hands. "What do you mean? I'm not even near you." He took a step toward me and I headed for the door connecting the classrooms.

I was just about to it when he grabbed me by

the back of the neck and maneuvered me to face him, crashing his lips into mine. My hands came up to shove against his chest, but instead, fisted his shirt as he backed me against the wall and pushed his tongue into my mouth.

My mind was screaming at me to push him away, but instead, I moved my tongue into his mouth and my knees weakened. If I had known kissing was so great, I would have found someone to make out with a lot sooner. Someone that wasn't paying someone to beat me up.

But maybe I was wrong and it wasn't him in particular. It seemed more like something Morgan would instigate. He was the one that was the notorious bad boy of the three.

He pulled away just enough so our lips were almost brushing. "You need to tell us where your father is."

My feelings of lust toward him evaporated and I shoved him, moving him back a few inches. "I don't know my father."

"I find that hard to believe." He crossed his arms over his chest, drawing my attention to how the button-up shirt he was wearing clung to his biceps and pecs.

He smirked and brought a hand to his mouth,

rubbing a finger over his bottom lip. I was distracted for a moment at how his lips seemed swollen from our kiss. Did mine look the same?

"Why is that hard to believe?" It was a struggle to keep my voice steady as my eyes tracked his every movement. "He left before I was one."

"Does your mom work?" He unbuttoned his sleeves and rolled them up to show his muscular forearms. "How does she make a living?"

I looked away to stop myself from ogling him. "What my mom does and doesn't do is none of your fucking business."

"I never pegged you for a girl that cusses." He stepped forward again. "By the way, where is your mom, Riley?"

My eyes met his and my heart stopped. Did he know where my mom was? I wracked my brain trying to remember if I had mentioned my mom going to the Maldives during the yearbook retreat. I opened my mouth to respond and then shut it.

"Here's what's going to happen." He trailed a finger down my jawline and I flinched away. "You're going to get your dad out of hiding."

"But-"

He pressed his forefinger to my lips. "Listen." I

nodded. "Once you make contact with him, you'll text me and I'll give you further direction."

Tears sprang to my eyes because I didn't have the faintest clue of how to get into contact with my estranged father. I had asked when I was younger about him and my mother had shut me down, telling me never to bring him up again.

He removed his finger and wrapped his hand around the side of my neck, bringing his forehead to mine. "Don't make this harder than it needs to be, Riley. There will be consequences."

He released me, and I sagged against the wall as he walked to the door. "Consequences? Like paying someone to jump me or putting fish in my dorm?"

He turned the door handle and paused, looking back over his shoulder. The look he gave me was enough to make me piss my pants. "You have seventy-two hours."

Chapter Four

RILEY

"Three days to get your father to contact you? Who the fuck does he think he is, a capo?" Ivy was pacing in my bedroom as I typed an email to my father's company email address.

I didn't know what else to do since my calls to all the corporate offices went unanswered and my mother was still not contacting me. I felt so alone, even with my friends having my back.

My mom had always been there for me when I needed her. It wasn't often I had to turn to her, but this entire situation warranted the intervention of a parent.

"I just want to wake up from this nightmare." Tears filled my eyes. "What if they did something to my mom? Why would he ask where she was if he didn't know?"

Ivy sat down on the edge of my bed. "I don't know. If he's looking for your father for whatever reason, maybe he tried calling her, or showed up here looking for her?"

I shook my head and stood, going to the window. "Maybe I should call the police."

"They can't take you away and put you in foster care or some shit, can they?" She came to stand next to me at the window. We could see a faint sliver of ocean between the townhouses. "You're almost eighteen."

"I don't know." I knew deep down that I should call the police, but my mom had said she'd be back next week. There was a multitude of reasons she might not be responding to my texts and calls. She could have poor reception or lost her cell phone. She lost her phone at least once a year.

Going to the police would make it all too real.

"Have you looked in her office and room for numbers? She has to have documents somewhere since he's giving her money, right?" Ivy's face grew determined and she went to my door. "If you aren't going to look, I will. I don't like this at all."

I had already thought of snooping, but was

putting it off. I wasn't the type of kid that went through my mom's stuff when she wasn't around. Just like she wasn't the type of mom that went through my stuff.

Of course, I never gave her any reason to snoop. Not that she'd find anything she didn't already know about if she did take a look around my room.

We started in the office that she seldom used. I sat down in the desk chair and looked at the photos of us over the years adorning the surface. I pulled open drawers and rifled through the contents, not finding much.

The files were filled with bills, receipts, and past tax returns; nothing with information about my father or his payments to her from what I could see.

"Did your mom have a recent boyfriend or anything?" Ivy finished opening and looking through some lower drawers on a bookshelf.

"You know how my mom is." *Natalia Hernandez Moreno doesn't need a man.* In my seventeen years, she hadn't brought any men home.

We left the office and entered my mom's bedroom. I didn't want to look in her nightstand drawers because I knew what I kept in *mine*, but we needed to look everywhere.

"Ew." Ivy slammed the drawer on the other side of the bed shut. "Do not look in this bottom drawer."

"I knew this was a bad idea." I opened the bottom drawer on the side I was on and frowned at the handgun and knife. "I didn't know my mom had a gun."

I picked up the knife and examined it. It looked like it was made of steel and the hilt had a swirling design made of abalone shell. It was gorgeous and should have been displayed, not shoved in a drawer.

"What was your mom going to do with that thing? Shank someone?" Ivy peered into the drawer. "Damn. Your mom doesn't seem like the type to shoot a gun."

I was too scared of accidently shooting myself to pick it up to see if it was real.

"Is there a type to own a gun?" I shut the drawer and set the knife on the top of the night-stand to grab later. "But you're right, I can't imagine her using it."

The closet was clean and organized. At first glance, nothing seemed amiss. I pulled on the top drawer of my mom's jewelry cabinet, not expecting it to open since it was usually locked. It was empty.

I frantically pulled out the other three drawers,

finding all of them devoid of the extensive jewelry collection. A lot of my mom's jewelry had been semi-precious, but she did have diamond pieces passed down to her.

"All of her jewelry is gone."

"Did your mom take the shoe boxes with her?" Ivy had her back to me and was staring at the empty shelves.

I hadn't even noticed when we walked in. I rushed to the corner of the closet and knew as soon as I pulled the first container from the shelf that it was empty. I opened it up and confirmed that all of her purses were gone.

My mom had sold everything.

***

IVY HAD OFFERED to spend the night, but I needed to be alone. For the last couple of days, I had been refusing to believe my mom could have run off, but now I needed to entertain the idea that she had.

What other explanation was there for her silence, the missing expensive belongings, and the missing money? But would my mom do that to me?

It had to have something to do with my dad and

the three assholes looking for him. I assumed Morgan was also, but he hadn't approached me at school yet.

I checked my phone for messages for the billionth time and stared at the ceiling. I still didn't understand why Jax would want me to contact my father. Was he mad about the lost sea life?

It angered me too, but I wasn't to blame for what happened. Maybe my inaction was what was angering him and I needed to step up and volunteer with an organization that helped the relief efforts.

My phone dinged and I swiped to open a text from Aiden.

Aiden: Miles just texted me and asked me on a date!

Me: What? That's amazing! About time he got his head out of his ass. You've liked him forever.

Aiden: Ivy told me what you found.

Me: I don't know what to do.

Aiden: I've been brainstorming all the ways your mom might know Jax's dad. They all grew up here, right?

Aiden sent me all his theories. Most of them were ridiculous, but one stood out. They might have known each other from high school. She never talked about high school and wasn't friends with anyone from when she was younger. All of her friends were transplants from other areas or went to Salinity Cove High at a different time.

I had none of my mom's friends' phone numbers to call. Not that they would know where she was, but they might know if she was dating someone without telling me. What if she had secretly been dating a woman and they ran off together?

I jumped up and ran up the stairs to the office to grab my mom's yearbooks. I sat down at the desk and went to the index to look up my mother. I wrote the pages on a sticky note so I wouldn't have to keep flipping back and forth.

She was on the swim team, and so was my father. I closed the freshman book and opened the next. I was starting to feel like it was a lost cause when I spotted a photo on the swim page with a guy that wasn't my father with his arm around my mom's neck, pulling her to him and kissing her cheek.

I went to the caption.

Finn West.

My eyes went wide and I went back to the freshman book, locating him. I started skimming through the comments written by friends on the inner cover and autograph pages and came across one written by Finn in the junior book.

Nat, I can't wait to spend the summer with you.

My mom hated being called Nat. There was no signature or note from my father. The senior book stared up at me and I wiped my hands on my shorts before opening it. After a few glasses of wine, my mom mentioned my father taking her to senior prom. She'd never once mentioned Finn West.

In the senior book, my mom wasn't even found on the swim team. The only picture I could find of her was her senior portrait. It was like she had stopped doing any activities.

It seemed like my mom had been with Jax's father, but sometime between junior and senior year, started going out with my father. It made no sense why Jax would be holding that against me.

I had to be missing something.

THE NEXT DAY at school was torturous, waiting to see what they would do next. A few fish comments still reached my ears, but both Blake and Jax were impassive toward me in our classes together.

At the end of the day, I went to my locker, and

inside was a folded note. *Forty-eight hours*. I shuddered and crumbled the paper before throwing it in the trash.

"Something wrong?" Morgan Wade, Salinity Cove's resident daredevil and playboy leaned against the locker next to me. "You look a little flushed."

He stroked my cheek with his knuckles and I pulled away. "Why are you assholes always touching me?"

His smile dropped as he thought about my question. "Why are you *letting* us touch you is the more important question."

He pushed off the locker and walked beside me as I headed to the parking lot. I should have answered him, but why waste my breath when they were on a mission to make me miserable?

"Did you need something?" I was comfortable confronting him since there was a school resource officer about fifty feet away.

"Can't a man walk a lady who is all by herself to her car?" He moved his motorcycle helmet into the opposite hand. "Wouldn't want anything *bad* to happen to you."

"I think I'll be fine." I sped up and stepped into the parking lot, careful to pay attention to anyone backing out. I'd had a few close calls. "Motorcycle parking is over there." I pointed without looking at him as he continued to follow me.

"Where are you going?" He stepped beside me again and I groaned.

I stopped walking and he turned to look at me. "It's none of your damn business where I'm going."

"Woah, there. I was just being polite. You should be grateful I'm by your side, protecting you from all these... cars." The shit-eating grin returned to his face and his hazel eyes twinkled with something unreadable. "Maybe we're headed to the same place."

"Doubtful." I purposely bumped into him as I passed him, making his hip bump against a car.

I now understood what drove people to beat the shit out of others. I was liable to punch one of them if they didn't leave me alone.

My car was my one safe haven where I could just drive away and forget about them. I took off toward the highway to head to my dance studio. For an hour, I could forget reality while I danced.

"Riley! Just the person I wanted to see!" My dance instructor, Bernardo, came around the counter and gave me a giant hug. "We might have finally found you a dance partner to compete with. He's coming in today, so go get dressed."

I instantly perked up. I loved competing on the amateur level, but always had to dance with an instructor. It was hard to find a partner around my age that could keep up with me. Teenage boys just didn't ballroom dance.

I quickly went to the bathroom to change into a skirt, tank, and my dance shoes. I touched up my make-up and redid my hair in a ponytail. As I slid the clasp on my shoe into place, I was hit with a reminder that I didn't have any money to pay for my lessons next month. My chest tightened as the reality of my situation sank in.

If my mom really had skipped town, I had no way of supporting myself. It was doubtful I'd get any help from the authorities since I was so close to adulthood, and the money in my college fund was only available for college.

A knock sounded on the door and I jumped. "Riley, your new partner is here." Bernardo lowered his voice. "He's hot."

I checked the mirror one last time and put my bag on the shelf in the corner before heading out to the dance floor.

Spotlight Studio was one of my favorite places

to be outside of school. It was a large, open room that had a smaller studio room that could be blocked off by curtains. The walls were lined with floor to ceiling mirrors, and at night, the florescent lights were turned off and the chandeliers were turned on.

It might just have become my favorite place now, since school had taken an unfortunate turn.

My mom had dragged me to an open house my freshman year. Despite her Mexican heritage, she liked to say the rhythm must have skipped a generation because she danced with two left feet and no hip action. Although I'd never met my grandma, my mom said she was lusted over by men all across Salina Cruz.

I hoped whoever this new guy was, he could move his hips, because that was a constant problem with the males. I almost just wanted to give up and go the female partner route.

Bernardo clapped his hands together in excitement as I approached the guy leaning on the counter. His back was to me, but he had disheveled dark hair that was cut short on the sides and a muscular-looking back. I couldn't help but look at his ass, which was just the right amount of plump.

I really hoped he could dance well.

"This is the lovely Riley Kline, one of our most promising young dancers." Bernardo waved his hand with a flourish in my direction as the man turned around.

I came to a halt and clenched my jaw to keep from crying out in frustration. What the hell was Morgan doing in *my* dance studio?

The smirk on his face said it all, and I cursed myself for mentioning ballroom dancing the day before to Jax. This had to be planned and a way to further make my life miserable.

"Riley Kline." He reached for my hand from its spot at my side and brought it to his mouth, kissing the back of it. Heat spread across my cheeks. "It's my pleasure."

What I really wanted to say was, "Cut the crap, you sadistic asshole," but instead, I said, "The pleasure is all mine."

Bernardo had his hands clasped at his chest and mouthed *oh my god* to me. He'd have kicked him to the curb if he knew what had been going on. Instead, he did Cha-Cha lock steps all the way to the stereo and plugged in his phone.

I cringed at the thought of my feet being assaulted. Morgan was a swimmer and had never shown any inkling that he could dance or had any rhythm. During junior year, he had stood on the lunch table and tried to twerk and sent everyone into a fit of laughter before the school resource officer told him to get down.

"Can you even dance?" *I've Got the World on a String* by Michael Bublé came over the speakers and I made no move to offer my hand to him. "This is ridiculous. Do you even know what dance this is?"

"I watched some videos and then had my first lesson yesterday." He stepped forward and his hand slipped under my arm and splayed across my shoulder blade. He put his lips next to my ear and a tingle went down my spine. "Foxtrot."

At least he knew where to put his hand.

"Great." I shut my eyes and breathed in deeply before giving him my right hand to hold in dance position. "Let's just get this over with so I can dance with a real dancer."

He pulled me flush against his body into closed hold, keeping his mouth against my ear. "You aren't a Back-Lead Betty, are you? I like to be in charge." He meant more than just in dance.

"Only when the lead doesn't know what he's doing." I took a step backward, pulling him with me.

We moved in time to the music and he took

over. He knew how to dance as if he'd been dancing since he was out of diapers. His lead was strong, and I relaxed as we flew around the dance floor.

The music cut off and Bernardo clapped. "Oh my Gucci! That was like butter. I can't wait to see Latin." He put his fist against his mouth and bit it. "And my boyvaries are already tingling at the thought of tango with you two."

Morgan being in my safe haven still made me feel queasy, but he could move. When dancing, that was the only thing on my mind.

The hour flew by, and when the lesson was done, Bernardo took us into one of the offices to chat. I was impressed with Morgan and his ability on the dance floor, but I didn't know what his angle was.

"From my vantage point, this is a match made in dance heaven." Bernardo pulled out a binder that had pricing in it. "The next competition for your age group and ability level is in three months in Hawaii. The question is, how much time do you want to devote?"

"I'm willing to devote whatever it takes." Morgan was relaxed in the chair next to me and took my hand.

I couldn't pull away, not when we had just been

dancing so intimately together. I looked down at his hand clasping mine and sighed.

"How much is it going to cost?" I didn't usually bat an eye at how much dancing and events cost, but I was wondering how I was going to buy food for the next week without asking Ivy.

Maybe I could sell some of my clothes or the ones my mom had left in her closet. The knife would probably fetch a nice amount at a pawn shop.

"The trip to Hawaii with hotel, flight, and all of your entrance fees will be around three thousand each." He pulled a calculator out of a drawer. "And with you two being a new partnership, I would recommend three lessons a week. That will be about twenty-five hundred a piece."

My eyes widened and I pulled my hand from Morgan's. I stood and backed toward the door. "I forgot I have somewhere to be. I'll call you later."

I rushed out and to the bathroom to grab my belongings. This was the reality check I needed. I was going to go straight to the police station and file a missing person's report.

I managed to make it into the parking lot when a hand took me by the elbow and spun me around. On instinct, I swung my hand to slap him, but he grabbed my wrist just before it was about to make contact.

"Aren't we feisty?" Morgan let my wrist go. "Why are you crying?"

I swiped at my cheeks and glanced at my car. "It's nothing." I tried to step past him and he blocked my path. "Move out of my way."

There were enough people around. All it would take was a scream to have them coming to my rescue. Hopefully.

He crossed his arms over his chest. "Not until you tell me what's wrong."

"What's wrong?" My voice came out with a squeak. "You assholes are stalking me, kissing and touching me without my permission, and threatening me!"

"I've never kissed you or threatened you." He shook his head. "Wait, who the fuck kissed you?"

I found it hard to believe that Jax didn't tell him about the two kisses he'd laid on me. One of which I could still feel. I didn't even know why I allowed it to happen or why I didn't kick him in the nuts.

I should have kicked him in the nuts. Next time I would. I shook my head at the image of him pressing against me, his lips covering mine as his hands roamed my body.

"I've done nothing to you three." I darted around him and jumped in my car.

Before I managed to shut the door, he stopped it with his hand and leaned down to look me in the eye. "One of my favorite games is hide-and-seek."

"Is that supposed to scare me?" Because it did, but it also excited me in a sick and twisted way.

He laughed. "There's only one way to get me to leave you alone." He shut my door, giving me a little finger wave before going back into the dance studio.

What the hell was I going to do and what the *fuck* was wrong with me?

Chapter Five

RILEY

*T*wenty-four hours.

I slammed my locker shut and pinched the bridge of my nose. *Maybe I should look into independent study until everything blows over.* I hadn't been able to focus at all in class thinking about my mom and the impending deadline set by the Tritons.

The evening before, I had gone to the police station, but they had been no help, saying that if my mom told me a date of return, I needed to wait until twenty-four hours after that date.

When I burst into tears, the officer took down some information and said he'd see what he could find out. I wasn't holding my breath.

Even worse, the morning news reported that,

after an investigation, it had been discovered that engineers on the oil platform had reported the need for necessary fixes to the oil wells, but they had fallen on deaf ears.

Where was Robert Kline in this whole mess? No one knew. He had taken his private jet and vanished. The Federal Aviation Administration was still investigating where the plane had gone.

"You know what you need?" Aiden appeared beside me and slung his arm around my shoulders. "A night of fun. You. Me. Ivy. This Friday. Football game. Bonfire."

I groaned. "And how is that fun? *They* will be there, won't they?" I pulled open the door to the aquatic center and stopped to look at him. "It's bad enough that I have to do the coverage on swimming."

We entered the lobby area of the state-of-the-art facility. Most of the major high school swim meets were hosted there because of it. Even the lobby was impressive, with a giant snack bar and sitting areas with big screens.

I thought it was a bit much, but the swimming program brought in big money, not only for our school, but the community as well. Finn West was also one of the donors that helped fund it being built.

"Why can't Jax do the swimming coverage?"

I took my camera out of my bag as we entered the main facility. The swim teams were already training and I had a hard time keeping my eyes off the shirtless, muscular male forms. "He can't take pictures while swimming. I hate to say this, but the main photos should probably be those three."

As we got closer, the Tritons glanced in my direction and then their heads went together. They hadn't been in the water yet, but it looked like they were just getting ready to go in.

"Girl, I can't tell if they just gave you the stank eye or bedroom eyes." He plopped into a cushioned chair. "They are fine though. Maybe their kink is being dominant alphas and they want you to fall to your knees in submission like an omega wolf."

"I think their kink is being utter assholes." I dropped my bag on the ground next to him. "Being hot isn't an excuse for the way they've been toward me. I don't care who they are or how much money they have."

They'd have to buy me a thousand roses and a five-carat diamond for me to even consider one of them. Not that any of them were interested in me.

They were just trying to mess with me and break me.

"Have you told them that?" Aiden cocked a brow and then smirked when I just stared blankly at him. "Be firm with them. Guys like them will take advantage of weakness in a heartbeat. Put them in their place."

I turned and moved closer to take photos. The yearbook had excellent cameras and zoom lenses for me to stay a safe distance from the pool. Even being close to it was making my breath hitch a little.

Swimming was one of the more difficult sports to get good shots of because of the water. I started snapping photos of the swimmers in the water and those standing around preparing to get in.

I zoomed in on the Tritons, who were still clustered together. Jax handed something to Morgan and he put it in his mouth. I held the button down to take burst shots, and not a second later, Jax handed the same thing to Blake.

Whatever had just happened, I had captured it, and an odd satisfaction washed over me. They surely wouldn't take drugs in plain sight, would they? Drugs would certainly explain how they dominated the pool like they did.

I stayed for another fifteen minutes before

calling it a day. I didn't need to stay for the whole practice. The real magic would come when they had a meet.

"WHAT DO you mean she turned her car in?" I clutched my phone in my hand and felt the instant need to throw up.

"She was leasing it and turned it in to the car dealership. They gave her a ride to the airport. They don't remember much other than she seemed sad. I'm going to reach out to the airlines tomorrow and see what they say. Do you know of anyone she had issues with?"

"No, but the oil spill..." I sighed and propped my elbow on the kitchen table where I had been working on an assignment. "There are some guys at my school who have been threatening me."

I filled in the detective on the past week and he said he was concerned. He suggested I speak to the administration or the school counselor so their parents could be contacted.

I'm sure that would go over well.

There was a reason they were called the Tritons. They were virtually untouchable. Their parents invested a lot of money into the school, including the upgrades to the facilities and to academic and sports programs. We were essentially a private high school without tuition.

After hanging up the phone, I checked my emails again, and the spam folder, to make sure I didn't miss an email from my father or someone at his company. I had tried every email available on the company's website, hoping it would make its way to him.

The doorbell rang, and I jumped in surprise. I considered not answering, but the doorbell sounded again. I went to the living room window and carefully lifted a blind slat to peek.

Blue eyes met mine, and I cursed. I backed away from the window and nearly fell over the arm of the couch. Why was Jax at my door and how did he know where I lived?

He rang the doorbell again and I went back to the dining room and grabbed my phone to send him a text.

Me: Leave me alone.

Jax: I need to talk to you.

Me: There's nothing to talk about. I'm calling the police.

I stood frozen for a minute and then walked as

quietly as humanly possible back to the window to peek out. My shoulders relaxed. He was gone.

I turned and screamed. Jax was standing in the middle of the living room with a triumphant smile on his face.

I darted around the coffee table away from him, but he seized my arm. I picked up the first thing I could get my hands on and hit him with it. The sound of plastic against bone made me flinch.

He let me go with a grunt and rubbed his jaw. "Fuck, Riley. I'm not going to hurt you." He snatched the television remote from me and threw it on the couch. "I just want to talk."

He stalked after me as I ran up the stairs to my room. I locked the door and quickly called back the number the detective had called me from.

"Detective Wilson speaking."

"He's in my house." I looked around my room and grabbed the knife I had taken from my mom's nightstand. "Please help me."

"Where are you?"

"In my bathroom, please hurry." I shut and locked my bathroom door and tried to stay calm.

Sure, I'd imagined something like this before after watching too many movies, but never did I think I'd be dealing with it myself. My body trembled and my skin felt sweaty and cold at the same time.

"Officers are on the way."

A knock sounded on the bathroom door and I gripped the knife. Why was he doing this to me? I bumped into the wall as I backed toward the shower.

"Riley." He drew out my name, taunting me. He jiggled the door handle.

If he could get into my bedroom that quickly, he would easily get into the bathroom. I was going to have to stab him.

"He's outside the bathroom door," I whispered, clutching the phone tight.

"Do you have something to protect yourself with? ETA is three minutes." I heard sirens from his end of the phone.

"I don't think I have three minutes." The lock turned and the phone slipped through my fingers, smashing into the tile floor as the door swung open.

I backed up into the shower and held the shaking knife in front of me. Jax bent to pick up the phone and ended the call to the detective.

His eyes went from the knife to my face. "Your back door was unlocked." He set the phone on the counter and met my eyes in the mirror. "Why don't you put the knife down, Riley."

"The police are coming." Probably not the smartest thing to say, but maybe he'd run. "Get out of my house."

He was standing at the shower door now, blocking any exit out of the predicament I was in. I should have gone to my mom's bedroom for her gun. It couldn't be that hard to shoot someone. There was a safety and then I just had to pull the trigger.

His eyes fell to the knife again and they narrowed. "Where did you get that knife?"

I didn't answer, my entire body stiff. If he came forward, would I be able to stab him? How hard would I have to jab him with it to cause injury?

He turned his head toward the door as if he was angling it to listen. He made a growling noise in his throat and then walked out without another word.

My body relaxed and I suddenly felt the need to sit down. I pushed into the tiled wall to keep from sliding to the shower floor. If he came back, I needed to be ready.

A few moments later, I heard the sound of sirens and then the front door being kicked in. I sagged against the wall and the knife clinked against the tile after slipping from my hand. I was safe.

Twenty minutes later, I was on the couch with a glass of water in my hands and a splitting headache. The adrenaline rush left me exhausted and weak.

"No signs of forced entry. I checked all the doors and windows and they were all locked." I sat, numb, on the couch as the detective filled out a report. Jax must have locked the back door when he left. "You're positive he was inside the house?"

"Yes." I furrowed my brows and looked inside my glass at the bubbles around the edge.

The detective's phone rang and he answered it, making nonverbal noises as the person on the other end talked to him. "The two officers that went to his house say he was in the middle of an extracurricular activity with a female."

I blinked so many times I thought my eyelids were going to ignite. "But that's impossible. It hasn't been that long. How could he get home and already be in bed with a girl?"

Detective Wilson leaned forward and put his clipboard on the coffee table before turning toward me with a sympathetic face. "Look... sometimes when the mind is under a lot of stress-"

I stood. "You think I made it up?" I couldn't

84

believe someone that should be on my side was questioning me.

"I think you are a smart young woman who is worried about her mother." He grabbed his clipboard and stood. "I will swing by and speak to Mr. West. I want to suggest that you call a friend to come spend the night or go to their house until we send someone out to fix your door tomorrow."

I decided his disbelief didn't warrant a thank you. I shut the door and pushed an oversized chair in front of it until I went to Ivy's.

None of this would be happening if it wasn't for my sperm donor.

Chapter Six

JAX

I want her.

Ever since she looked up at me with her emerald green eyes and uttered *excuse me* she was all I could think about.

My task had been simple; distract her long enough for Blake and Morgan to get into her dorm room that night and leave a very clear message. A message that was meant to get back to her father. She hadn't even connected that dead fish insinuated swimming with the fish in death.

Instead of going to plan, my lips had found hers and my fingers ached to feel the heat between her legs. There was something about her that drew me to her and I wanted to make her mine, but she'd stopped me. No one ever stopped me.

I leaned on the railing at the edge of our cliff and looked out at the glistening ocean in the moonlight. I shut my eyes and imagined slicing through the water at top speeds and swimming alongside my aquatic friends. It had only been three days since I'd been in the ocean, but my skin itched for a swim and my heart ached for the companionship of the other creatures that called the ocean home.

"Are the police taken care of?" Blake interrupted my fantasy and I turned toward him, leaning my forearms back against the railing.

Morgan stood shoulder to shoulder with Blake, both of their eyes shooting daggers at me. I'd fucked up again.

I should have dived right off the cliff to avoid the conversation that I'd already had with myself. I was supposed to run point on this assignment and had fucked up several times already. I couldn't help that my lips craved the taste of hers or that my broken heart muddled my thoughts.

I had one job. Scout out her house and see where possible entry points were. There was an alarm, but it wasn't operational. A quick call to the alarm company that Blake's father had investments in confirmed that.

"They bought it." I turned back to the ocean

and felt them come to stand behind me. "I've got it under control."

All it had taken was ripping my shirt off and unbuttoning my pants to have the cops believe I had been fucking a girl. They wouldn't dare question me, not when our families were so deeply entrenched in their livelihood at the Salinity Cove Police Department.

"Do you?" Blake leaned on the railing and looked at me with concern in his eyes. I was tired of them looking at me like that. "Bro, you broke into her house."

My jaw ticked at his condescending tone and I didn't speak. It was true. I had let my emotions get the best of me. There was something about her that captivated me and refused to let go, even though she was the last person I should want.

I hadn't had the intention of entering her house or even making my presence known, but she had a pull over me I couldn't explain. Ever since I'd kissed those soft pink lips of hers, I'd wanted more.

When I had walked around the townhouse to the small backyard, I saw her through the sliding glass door at the front window, peering out. The front of the house had nowhere to hide a spare key, but the back had plenty. It was easy to find.

"Did you forget the other reason why we're doing this?" Morgan put his hand on my shoulder. "Maybe we're due for a trip to see your sister."

I shook my head and headed back toward the large sliding doors that spanned the entire living area of the house. I didn't want to think about my sister and didn't need to see her to remember why my father was so hell bent on finding Robert Kline and making him pay. "I'm going for a swim."

Riley claimed to not even know Robert, and while that might have been true, he was still her father. A father wouldn't just let his daughter suffer, would he? He'd come to save his little girl if we pushed her enough. My own father was certain of it.

"We need to tread carefully with this girl." Morgan shoved his hands in his pockets and followed me inside. "That includes keeping your lips off her."

"Wait a fucking second. You kissed her?" Blake was pissed. I was pissed at myself for having no self-control. "When?"

"At the yearbook retreat." I headed toward the elevator, but Blake stepped in front of me. "And Monday after class." Plus, I thought about it multiple times while jacking off and in my dreams. Oh, and anytime I saw her.

"I thought we agreed not to take things there. I mean, shit, she is cute as hell, but we can't... I mean, can we?" Blake put his hands on his hips and then a grin spread across his face. "Maybe we should take it there. I bet she's a virgin."

"We?" I clenched my fists and resisted the urge to punch him in the gut. We might have been close, but that didn't make them immune to getting the beat down if it needed to happen. "I'm not sharing her."

"Then stop fucking kissing her." Blake stepped out of the way. "We'll go see your sister. I'll put a call in for us."

"I don't need to see my sister."

"We're supposed to be proving we're ready." Morgan's reminder felt like a kick to my balls. "We need to keep our eyes on the prize."

I pressed the button and the elevator dinged open. They followed me inside and we stood in silence as it descended to sea level. We stepped out into the cave and started removing our clothes.

"She has a knife that looks an awful lot like a siren's." I had considered not telling them about it because I wasn't one-hundred percent sure it had been real. It *couldn't* have been real.

"Excuse me?" Morgan's eyes went wide as he folded his pants and put them on a bench. "How?"

"I didn't get that good of a look at it, but I swear I saw abalone insets on the hilt. She had her fist pretty tightly wrapped around it." I rubbed the back of my neck. "That would be impossible though."

"I'd have to see it." Blake stood at the edge of the platform. "It's doubtful it's real."

I stood next to him. "I hope you're right." Because if it was real, we needed to worry about where she got it.

Morgan was practically vibrating standing on the edge of the platform. "We can't go this long again. It hurts to shift."

Our house sat on a cliff overlooking the ocean, and in the cliff was a hollowed-out section with boats and jet skis. With a push of a button, the cliff opened to the wide-open sea. There was also an exit under the water for us to swim through.

"Stop being a guppy." Blake dove into the water, his body instantly morphing as soon as his fingertips hit the surface.

Morgan whooped and dove in after him.

Even if I did want to kiss Riley more, she would

never accept this world. Humans could never know of our existence, which was the entire purpose of some of us being on land in the first place. With tritons being entrenched in the human world, we could squelch any discovery of our existence.

I dove off the platform and the change ripped through me, my legs burning as the connective tissue grew. Morgan was right about it being uncomfortable. Freshman year we could only go a day without changing.

With swimming practice three days a week, the urge to shift was strong. Only true tritons from an elite bloodline could manage to keep the human appearance for as long as we could, and even then it took years of training to work up to a solid week of being bipedal.

Blake and Morgan stared back at me under the water with their amber-colored eyes. Our eyes were similar to a feline's which allowed for quick adjustment of the pupil underwater.

I swam toward the exit of the cave and then we were free. My mind and body became relaxed as we raced out to sea.

Chapter Seven

RILEY

*A*fter the night I had, I knew I would be struggling to focus all day. It didn't help that Blake was in my first three classes. If Jax was willing to break into my house and scare me half to death, how far were Blake and Morgan willing to go?

"Do you hear that?" Blake scooted his chair over so he was closer. "That's time, ticking away. *Tick, tick, tick.*"

I clenched my teeth and refused to look up from the response I was writing. I had been trying to ignore him and was reaching my limit. I hadn't gotten much sleep and felt like my head was going to explode.

Blake snatched my pen and held it away from

me when I tried to grab it back. I grunted out my frustration and reached into my bag to grab another pen. As soon as my pen hit my paper, it was snatched from my grip.

"Ms. Williams." I raised my hand. Once I had her attention, I gestured to the thorn in my side. "Blake is taking my pens."

A few heads turned, but most of the class was focused on the short answer prompt we were answering from the reading the night before. Reading I had skimmed because dealing with police and a broken door took time.

"He took your pen? What grade are we in?" She crossed the room so she wasn't talking across it and gave Blake a pointed look that said he was disturbing her normally peaceful class. "Give her back her pens."

"She said I could borrow them." Blake's frown was almost believable. "I can't help that she's PMSing and changed her mind."

A few females gasped around the room and one of the guys in front of us shook his head and shot Blake a sympathetic look.

Mrs. Williams rubbed at her eyebrow. "You are eighteen years old. Give her the pens."

I sat up straighter in my chair as she walked

away and Blake threw them onto my desk. "Six hours, Kline."

He grabbed his own pen and started writing without another word. My hand shook as I picked it up and tried to finish conveying my thoughts. It was hard to concentrate when his words echoed in my ears.

The sounds of the clock ticking didn't help. It was a constant reminder that time was running out and I didn't have what they wanted.

At the end of the period, Mrs. Williams asked me and Blake to stay behind. I didn't want to hear the ridiculous lies Blake was about to spin. He liked to bullshit.

"What's going on with you two?" She leaned against her desk as we both stood near the front row of desks. "Every day this week there has been something and it's becoming a disruption. Blake, starting tomorrow, you're going to sit elsewhere."

He crossed his arms over his chest. "Why do I have to change seats? She's the one causing the issue."

I resisted the urge to roll my eyes and stayed quiet. It was a lost cause where he was concerned. Anything I said would be contorted to a new story that met his needs. He had shown just how good of a manipulator he was over the past week.

"You are changing seats because I want you to." She moved around her desk and straightened some papers. "You are seniors. You need to start acting like it. Now, if there's nothing else, I need to get ready for my next class."

Blake stalked out of the classroom, pushing open the door harder than necessary. I jumped as it hit the wall outside.

"Riley. Is everything okay?" Mrs. Williams sat in her chair and laced her fingers under her chin. "I'm always here to talk or I can request Mrs. Miller pull you out of next period."

"I'm fine." I stuck a fingernail in my mouth and then shook my head, realizing I was about to bite the nail off. I had stopped biting my nails ages ago. "I think moving his seat will help."

She looked at me with her lips pressed in a line. "Just know that my door is always open."

I thanked her and left the room, glancing at my phone. It was becoming an obsession, checking my phone for messages or emails. I needed to find out what the Tritons knew about my mother.

The second the door shut, my phone was

plucked from my fingers. I didn't even have time to try to grab it.

"You shouldn't be alone with a teacher in a classroom. People might get the wrong idea." Blake turned and started to walk away with my phone before he turned to walk backward. "I'd totally be down to watch that though. Mrs. Williams is top of the line MILF."

"You're disgusting." I grabbed my phone back and, thankfully, he let me. Our fingers brushed and he stopped my retreat by grabbing my wrist.

He looked down where he touched my skin and cocked his head to the side. "Do you feel that?"

Did I feel the heat from our connection? Of course I did. Anyone would have a reaction when someone touched them unannounced and without provocation.

"Stop touching me. I didn't give you permission."

He let me go and smiled. I hated when he smiled because it made him look like the sweetest person in the world. His teeth were shockingly white against his brown skin, and I couldn't keep my eyes off his face.

"How about this." He followed me as we

headed to our next class. "You tell us where to find your father and I'll stop touching you."

I stopped and he bumped into me. He grabbed my arms and steadied me. I wrenched my body away and turned to poke him in the chest.

"I don't know." I punctuated each word with a stab of my finger. "Why do you care anyway?"

He took my hand and then placed his over mine on his chest. "You wouldn't understand."

I scoffed and yanked my hand from his, the loss of contact causing me to shiver. He noticed and smirked. "You do feel it."

The bell rang and I slipped into the classroom, wondering if I should just call it a day and ditch.

———

WAITING for your reckoning is never easy, and as the day drew to a close, my insides twisted into a painful knot. It felt like I'd eaten a bad street taco. I only wished that was what caused the tightness in my belly.

I tried to distract myself by working on a layout, but instead, watched Jax sitting in front of me. He hadn't even looked at me as he entered the room and took his seat. Today, he didn't try to get Tory to move, which was a change from the norm.

My shoulders were so tense they were practically touching my ears, and I checked my phone under the table for the hundredth time, waiting for something to happen.

It was seventy-one hours and forty-five minutes since the demand had been issued.

Jax stood from his seat and walked to the front of the room. I gripped the edge of the table, my knuckles turning white. Tory glanced over at me but didn't say a word as she looked between me and Jax.

Jax asked Mr. Garcia something and then left the classroom. I let out a breath, my hands loosening on the table.

"What was that about?" Tory whispered.

I shook my head and then my eyes widened before I dropped to the floor like I was picking something up. Tory didn't say a word as I crawled under the desk and reached as far as I could under the back and yanked Jax's backpack to me.

She shook her head and a smile played at the corner of her lips. She turned back to her computer. I unzipped the front pouch and scrunched my nose at the condoms and then rummaged inside.

I probably had less than a minute until he came back from the bathroom. I brought a bottle of pills out of a small compartment in the front pocket. There was no label, and they looked like pain relievers. I opened the lid and Tory made a noise of disapproval.

I tapped one out into my palm, shoved it in my pocket, and replaced the bottle and his backpack. I had just scooted my chair up to the desk when Jax came back in the room.

Sweat beaded his brow and I wondered if he had just used one of his condoms. I knew what went on in the bathrooms outside the science wing during seventh period. Everyone except the adults did. If he had just fucked someone, that was rather quick.

"What are you doing?" Tory scooted her chair close. "What was that?"

"I don't know." I clicked out of my files and shut down the computer. "But I'm going to find out."

The bell rang and Jax left like there was a fire under him. He was probably lying in wait like a hunter stalking its prey right outside the classroom door.

I steeled my resolve and left the room. I looked in the breezeway between the building I was in and the next over and saw nothing out of sorts. I walked cautiously to my locker, bracing myself for the inevitable.

I opened my locker and a white piece of paper was inside. I needed to tape something over the vents so they couldn't shove anything else through.

Time's up.

It didn't seem like anything could be worse than them inserting themselves into my life and Jax breaking into my house. They were psychopaths, and I realized that I was going to have to get concrete evidence for any adult to do anything.

Ivy rushed over to me as I was closing my locker. From the panicked look on her face, what she was about to tell me was what I had been waiting for all week.

"Just tell me." I raised my hands in frustration and they smacked against my legs as I let them fall. I didn't know what could be worse than breaking into my house and getting away with it.

"It's your car."

I pushed past her and she jogged behind me as I speed-walked to the parking lot. I came to a stop at the gate, seeing the crowd surrounding my car with their phones out. As if knowing I had arrived, the crowd parted as I walked toward them.

"I feel sorry for her."

"All the dolphins are dying."

"I heard a whale washed up on shore this morning."

"Her family are murderers."

The words assaulted my ears and I bit down on the flesh just below the inside of my lip. My eyes stung as I held back the tears that wanted to escape. I unlocked my car and slid inside.

Fuck them.

Even as I revved the engine, students continued to block my car that was now smeared with some kind of red substance that looked like blood. That wouldn't have bothered me.

The word *murderer* written across the white hood did, though.

I laid on my horn and they finally moved out of the way as I slowly backed up. By some miracle, I made it out of the parking lot without hitting anyone. If I had seen the Tritons, I would have run them down.

Too embarrassed to go to a carwash, I headed home and pulled to a stop in the driveway. I put my head on my steering wheel and turned off my car.

This was only the beginning.

I CHECKED every single window and door in the entire house after washing my car and calling to cancel my dance lesson. I only had four lessons left on my account before I needed to pay for more. The thought saddened me, but I was more concerned if the power was about to be turned off.

I locked myself in my bedroom since the security system was no longer functioning thanks to my mother not paying the bill since June. I had even removed all of the little metal keys on top of all the door frames.

I opened my nightstand drawer and stared at the gun I had moved from my mom's room. I had no clue how to use it, but I felt safer with it next to me.

YouTube showed all I needed to do was flip the safety, aim, and fire. I could at least use it as a threat. It was easier said than done, but it would have to do.

I sat at my desk and opened my laptop. The pill I had taken from Jax's backpack sat in a baggie and I examined it again. There was a trident symbol engraved into it. There were no pharmaceuticals on the market with such a marking, but there was an illegal drug that was a different color with the same symbol.

I slammed the screen shut in frustration and picked up my phone. I had refused to look at it after the strawberry jam that had been dumped on my car. I was sure social media was in a frenzy over it.

I pulled open my texts and my breath sped up. I wanted to throw my phone out the window, but I needed to be proactive and try to stop whatever they were going to do next.

Jax: It's only just begun. You know what you need to do.

Me: Get a restraining order?

Jax: What for?

Me: How'd you get in my house?

Jax: I wasn't in your house.

He was definitely smart and wasn't about to admit in writing he broke in. I set my phone down and changed into an oversized t-shirt before crawling into bed. I stared at the chain of texts and bit my lip.

Me: I know your secret.

The message was read, but he didn't reply.

Good. Let him sweat a little.

Chapter Eight

I had never been so happy for it to be Friday. Had my mom been home, I would have asked her to call me in sick. The last thing I wanted was Saturday detention for an unexcused absence.

I sat in the guidance counselor's office, staring across the desk at her as she tapped her pen. "Your teachers and a few students have expressed some concerns over what has gone on this week."

I looked down at my hands folded in my lap and my cheeks puffed as I exhaled. "You could say it's been a rough week."

Most of my classmates didn't say or do anything per se, but they stared. A lot. They were just as guilty becoming bystanders instead of allies. I had been guilty of the same, telling myself it was none of my business and fearing the bullies would come after me. This was a rude awakening.

I didn't even want to think about what social media looked like. I had stayed off all the apps all week. The last thing I needed was another thing to worry about.

"What does your mom think about all of this? Have you told her?" The pen stopped tapping and I looked up and met Mrs. Miller's concerned eyes. "Bullying is not okay, but we can't do anything if you don't tell us who is doing it."

I twisted my lips to the side and remained silent. I should have told her, but was nervous I'd have a mental breakdown if I rehashed everything. Would it even help? The Tritons ran the school.

After a tense minute of silence, I looked past her and out into the quad her office window over-looked. "Jax West, Blake Huron, and Morgan Wade."

If she was surprised, she didn't show it. "You should report every incident so myself or Mr. Lee can investigate. We checked the video footage, but there were technical issues." She opened her drawer and then slid a small pack of M&Ms across to me.

"Technical issues?" I stared at her, not believing

for a second that the cameras just happened to be inoperable. "Even if I did report them, what good would that do? They're the Tritons."

I took the candy and opened it. I needed a king-size bag after this week. I closed my eyes as the chocolate melted on my tongue.

"Is that what they're calling themselves?" She snorted. "Do they realize they're calling themselves mermaids?"

I laughed along with her before my laughter faded and I played with the small wrapper in my hands. "My mom took everything and left. The police won't do anything until twenty-four hours after she told me she'd return."

I looked up through my eyelashes, and Mrs. Miller's eyebrows drew together. A deep frown slid into place, which made her look ten years older. "Your mother wouldn't leave you like that."

"I'm almost eighteen. I know she was pretty upset about the whole oil platform thing. Maybe it was too much." I tilted my head back and dumped the rest of the fun-sized bag into my mouth.

Mrs. Miller stood and went to a file cabinet and used a key on her lanyard to unlock it. She opened the bottom drawer and pulled a file from the back. She sat back down with a heavy sigh.

I swallowed the last of the chocolate and stared at the folder that looked like it had seen better days. "What's that?"

"I was a year ahead of your mother in high school. When I got a job here, I found this cleaning out the files. The counselor in this office before me kept everything. Forty years of everything." She opened the manila folder and took out a piece of paper. "It's a police report of an assault on Robert Kline by Finn West. Charges were dropped."

I reached forward and took it. "I saw in my mother's junior yearbook she was cozy with Finn, but she went to senior prom with my dad."

Mrs. Miller laced her fingers under her chin. "Your dad stole your mother from Finn. Finn and Natalia had been together since freshman year. They were the couple everyone was jealous of."

The police report didn't tell me much other than Finn West beat the shit out of my father at the beginning of senior year. "Why would Jax and his friends torment me for this though?"

"I'm not sure." There was a knock on the door and the head school resource officer walked in. "Riley, this is Officer Thomas. I want you to seek him out whenever you have trouble with those three."

I looked up at the officer and smiled. He didn't return the sentiment and crossed his arms over his chest. I stood and handed Mrs. Miller the police report.

"I should get back to class." I grabbed my bag. "I'll find Officer Thomas if they bother me again."

I took the late note she handed me and slipped past the officer, not liking how he looked at me. Why was everyone a dick when there was no reason to be?

English was almost halfway over by the time I showed up. As soon as I entered the room, whispers erupted and I tried not to let my anxiety show on my face. I scanned the room quickly and didn't see Blake.

Once I slid into my seat, Aiden reached across and patted my hand, giving me a look that said he was on my team. I was glad I had Aiden and Ivy by my side.

The Tritons were all absent from school, which was relieving but worrisome at the same time. Maybe they had admitted to vandalizing my car and were suspended. I was pretty certain that was where Jax had gone at the end of yearbook the day before.

We sat down in the cafeteria after much discussion of the pros and cons of entering gossip central. The Tritons weren't around and it was our opportunity to see the rest of our friends. We weren't a big group that hung out, but any extra support I could get was a win.

"I can't believe they're targeting you. They're a bunch of assholes." Piper had been the most excited to see us eat in the cafeteria after we had avoided it all week. She wasn't a stranger to being bullied herself and went through a rough patch in junior high.

"Hot assholes." Santina looked over her shoulder at their table. "I'm missing my daily eye-candy today."

I laughed because Santina was a lesbian. She swore it was because penises looked like they had the eye of Mordor.

"I've got some eye-candy right here." Alex elbowed her. "I don't see why they are so popular. They don't do anything except swim."

Ivy began ticking reasons off on her fingers. "They're rich, mysterious, have amazing bodies, and I hear they are amazing lovers."

A chip went down the wrong way and I coughed, tears springing to my eyes. All eyes were on me as I took a swig of Sprite and shook my head. "How can high schoolers possibly know what good sex is?" This wasn't a romance novel.

"If you have enough of it." Aiden looked to their table and put his cheek on his fist. "I bet Miles is an amazing lover."

"I do not need to hear about your sexual conquests." Alex laughed. "You're really thinking about going after him?"

"He asked me out." Aiden grinned and did a little finger wave to Miles, who was looking in our direction. "If he wants to test the waters and explore his sexuality with me, I'm fine with that."

I missed the lunch crew we ate with. It was yet another thing that had been missing from my life over the past few days. I needed to find normal again, or as close to normal as possible.

I'd never felt like I needed to hide away and never come out again, but the last several days it had been temping to just stop caring.

My day was really starting to look up, but then the three of them walked into the cafeteria and headed straight for our table.

"Fuck." Ivy stood and put herself between them and the table. My best friend was badass to her core.

"Move out of the way, Ariel-reject." Morgan

glared around her at me. "Unless you want to be next."

If I could have seen her face, I'm sure she would have rolled her eyes. "Listen, fish boys, I don't know who you think you are-"

In the next second, Jax was around her and pulling me to my feet. "Come with us. Now." I didn't want my arm pulled off, so I stood.

The entire cafeteria had gone silent. Where the hell were the SROs? They should have been in the cafeteria doing their job. There were usually two during lunch that kept the peace.

"She isn't going anywhere with you." Aiden stood and pulled me away from Jax and put me behind him. "Go pick on someone else."

Jax narrowed his eyes. For a second, I thought a fight was going to break out, but then Jax backed up a step. "You'll regret this."

"I can't wait," Aiden deadpanned as they walked out of the cafeteria.

As soon as they were gone, the noise reached deafening levels, and I wanted to bury my head in the sand.

I sat back down and stared at my half-eaten food. "Thanks, guys. That was pretty-"

"Murderer. Murderer. Murderer." The chanting

started from the far side of the cafeteria where the Tritons crew sat and got louder and louder.

My face was probably as red as Ivy's hair as I ran for the nearest exit. I'd rather run than have them see my cry.

I ran right into a brick wall of a body and almost fell back. "Officer Thomas. They-"

He laughed and shoved past me just before Ivy and Aiden came out of the cafeteria. I stood gaping as he walked into the cafeteria, the chanting filtering out and then cutting off as the door shut.

I shut my eyes and held up a hand as Aiden started to talk. "I need to get out of here."

"We'll come with you." Ivy's voice was shaking.

"Alone."

I walked as fast as I could to the nearest bath-room and shut and locked the main door. I didn't hear anyone inside and a sob escaped me.

I needed to find my father.

———

"COME ON, Riley. Please don't lock yourself away like this." Ivy stood at the end of my bed where I was curled under the covers. "They want to break you, but you can't let them."

"Easy for you to say, they haven't done shit to you." My words were muffled by the pillow my face was buried in.

"Ivy's right." Aiden laid down next to me and yanked the comforter and pillow away from me. "When I came out in junior high, do you remember what happened?"

I rubbed my swollen eyes. "Yes."

"I could have locked myself back in my closet, but instead, I embraced it, and soon enough only a few assholes were calling me a faggot." Aiden stroked my hair. "So let's get you dressed and looking fierce. We'll show those idiots that you are a queen."

I snorted back a laugh. "I'm scared."

Ivy came out of my closet and threw two hangers on the bed. "What's the worst they could do? If they were going to physically hurt you, they would have already."

"Even the police are on their side." I pulled my bottom lip between my teeth. "They could murder me and get away with it."

I had fallen headfirst down a deep, dark hole of what-ifs when I got home from school. I was letting them win instead of putting a stop to their madness.

It wasn't like I had a choice in the matter. It was three against one.

"No." Aiden stood and took a red lace bra from Ivy. "Jax has kissed you twice. He might hate you for whatever reason, but that boy desires you."

I scrunched my nose and sat up. "It's all just a game."

"Then beat him at his game. Go after one of his friends." Aiden laughed and twirled the bra around his finger. "Turn them against each other."

"You want me to seduce one of them?" I couldn't help it, I laughed at that. "It's not a bad idea, though. Maybe I can get some information out of one of them."

Ivy practically skipped over to the bed and grabbed my hands, yanking me to my feet. "You can ask Morgan to dance with you and give Jax a show he won't forget!"

"I don't know... that will probably make the situation worse, won't it?" I snatched the bra from Aiden as it almost hit me.

"Maybe, but he'll also be pissed at Morgan." Ivy ushered me into the bathroom. "Take a shower and we'll do your hair and make-up."

"This isn't one of those high school dramas you

like to watch. Besides, I literally have no sex appeal."

"Honey, I'm gay, and I even know that is false. Just because you don't see it, doesn't mean others don't." Aiden plopped down on the bed and pulled out his phone. "Now hurry up, you hussy, we have men to seduce."

My common sense told me going to the senior bonfire to flirt with Morgan was a bad idea, but if I could distract him, there might be an opportunity to get information out of him. And maybe Ivy and Aiden were right. Maybe they would turn against each other.

It wouldn't hurt to try.

Chapter Nine

*T*he parking lot for the cove was almost full by the time we arrived. The town of Salinity Cove got its name from the crescent-shaped inlet that was sheltered from the wind and provided a private setting for shenanigans.

It was surrounded by cliffs, and the only way to get to it was through a three-foot wide path. During the day, it was a hotspot for families looking to escape the world for a bit, but at night, teenagers and young adults used it to party.

It was a tradition in our town to have bonfires most Fridays during football season. There was always alcohol and teenagers in compromising positions. It wasn't my scene, but it was where the Tritons hung out.

Aiden took my arm as we neared the path between the rocks that led to the beach. Melissa and a guy named Jacob stood at the entrance with their arms crossed over their chests.

"Are they supposed to be security?" Aiden snorted and stopped when Melissa blocked our path.

She looked me up and down before pulling out her phone to text something. I didn't need to see it to know she had just told the Tritons I had arrived.

"Can you move?" Ivy put a hand on her hip and glared at Melissa. "We don't live in Riverdale."

I laughed at the comparison. Ivy reminded me of Cheryl Blossom with her red hair and feisty, no bullshit attitude.

Melissa looked at her phone again. "You two can go in, but this one can't." She pointed to me and smirked. "Tritons' orders."

"Let's go, guys." I turned to walk away and ran straight into Jax.

Jax had his hands shoved in his jeans and his dark blue button-down shirt was rolled up to his elbows. He looked like he was going to a cocktail party or a happy hour, not a bonfire at the cove.

"What's the problem here?" His blue eyes sliced into me and left me feeling filleted open. He was so unbelievably gorgeous with his sharp jaw and five o'clock shadow that I almost forgot who he was.

"Your enforcers here aren't letting me on a *public* beach." I backed up a step because the woody citrus smell of his cologne was about to make me drool.

His head tilted to the side and his eyes moved down my body. My hair was down and curled to perfection by Aiden. It was longer than I usually liked, falling just below my shoulder blades, but he had trimmed the ends to make it not feel as weighed down. My make-up was simple, but Ivy had insisted on a deep red lip gloss that made my lips look amazing.

Even I had to admit I looked hot.

"Let her in." Jax brushed past me and disappeared down the path.

We got to the bottom of the path and took in the shoreline, lined with bonfires and high school students laughing, dancing, and making out. We walked across the sand toward the biggest bonfire.

"He's already spotted you," Aiden said in my ear. "It's those pants. They hug your curves like a second skin."

I stopped, and Aiden and Ivy gave me questioning stare. "I don't know if I can do this."

The whole thing felt sleazy to me and was

begging for something to go wrong. I never flaunted my body unless I was dancing. It wasn't that I was embarrassed with the curve of my hips or the roundness of my ass, but I didn't want to be objectified by horny teenage boys.

"Sure you can. You're already doing it without even trying. Honestly, I'm surprised you owned a pair of jeans that fit you this tight." He smacked my ass playfully as we started walking again. "Just turn on your inner siren."

I rolled my eyes and pulled at my black long-sleeve top that had a deep V-neckline showing a hint of my red lace bra. It was sending the wrong message, but to get their attention maybe that was what I needed. "My mom bought me these pants."

"Well, your mom is a smart woman. She knows a well-dressed tush is all you need to make that push." Aiden and Ivy separated from me as we stepped into the throng of partiers.

There were three bonfires spread out along the beach of the cove and most had music blaring and alcohol flowing. I spotted the Tritons, surrounded by their crew and a gaggle of girls dressed in skirts, shorts, and bikini tops that left little to the imagination.

I was way too overdressed.

Jax already had a girl on his lap and met my eyes from the other side of the flames. He looked like he wasn't having the greatest time, but a second later he was kissing the girl's neck as she threw her head to the side and giggled.

Blake had a girl on either side of him, his arms wrapped around their waists. He let one of them pour a shot in his mouth and tipped his head back. He was dressed in sweatpants and a white t-shirt that showed how powerful his upper body was. He was dressed like he didn't give a shit, or he just knew that he could wear lederhosen and girls would still fall at his feet.

Morgan was standing near the fire with his arms crossed, chatting with Miles, one of the other top swimmers of the school. If the Tritons weren't around, Miles would have been the top swimmer. I didn't quite understand why he'd asked Aiden out. He'd had a girlfriend at the end of junior year.

Morgan looked like he had just gone to a biker rally. He wore distressed dark jeans, leather boots, and a tight black shirt under a leather jacket.

Jax's eyes narrowed the closer I walked to the bonfire. A wave of confidence washed over me knowing he was watching me. He stood as I stopped next to Morgan.

"I'll only race that asshole if he lets us examine his bike first. Last time he almost beat me and I'm pretty sure he had a mod on it." Morgan still had his attention on Miles, but as soon as Miles looked at me, he turned his head. "Can I help you?"

His eyes landed on my lips before moving down to my chest and then down the rest of my body. I slipped my hands in my back pockets, making my chest more prominent.

You can do this.

"I want to dance." I parted my lips slightly and wet my lips. Morgan's eyes moved back to them.

"You want to dance?" He uncrossed his arms and turned toward me. He looked over my shoulder and then a grin spread across his face. "Okay, vixen. Let's dance."

Vixen was better than murderer.

He led me to where a mass of bodies was dancing. He pulled me flush against him and we began swaying to the music. It wasn't like on the ballroom floor when we could actually move our feet; we were limited because of the sand.

He put his mouth against my ear over my hair. "Jax is going to kick my ass. I hope you appreciate me sticking my neck out like this."

"Consider it repentance for all the shit you've

done to me." I slipped my arms around his neck and tried to keep my body from touching his without much luck. "Where'd you learn to dance?"

"I told you. YouTube." He smirked. "You can learn anything off there."

I rolled my eyes and he moved his hands right above my back pockets. "Where were you three today?"

"Aren't we nosy?" His eyes sparkled in the firelight. I couldn't stop my stomach from fluttering. "We were dealing with some oil spill aftermath."

My stomach turned sour and I tried backing away, but he tightened his hold on me. "Let me go."

"You wanted to dance." He turned me so we were both facing where Jax had returned to his spot perched on a log, glaring at me.

Something about his glare excited me more than it should have. I didn't know why these three guys made my body have a reaction. It was probably because I was a hormonal teenager.

Morgan's hands were on my hips as we moved to the music. "You weren't at the football game tonight."

My body trembled as he slipped his hands into my front pockets and hooked his thumbs in my belt loops. "I was getting ready."

"Whatever you're up to... I like it." His fingertips dug into my thighs and I tried not to react.

I hadn't wanted to believe Ivy and Aiden about Jax wanting me, but the proof was right in front of me as he balled his fists on his thighs as he watched us dance. Even with a girl hanging off him, his eyes were locked on me.

"Move your hair out of the way for me, vixen." Morgan's purr interrupted my thoughts.

My body was on fire, and not from the heat of the flames nearby. I wanted to run away, and I would have, but my body refused to do anything except stay plastered to his front.

I moved my hair to one side. His fingertips dug into my upper thighs again, closer to my apex. I put my hands over his and pushed down on his hands, causing him to groan.

His lips lowered to just under my ear. "You are so incredibly irresistible." His breath tickled my neck and my nipples tingled as they hardened. "It fucking sucks."

His lips brushed against my neck and my skin exploded in goosebumps. Jax was scowling and pulled a blonde into his lap, sliding his hand up her thigh and under the short fabric of her dress. His eyes were locked on mine as he let her kiss him, her tongue immediately probing at his lips.

I shut my eyes so I didn't have to watch.

"Let's go to the parking lot." Morgan took a handful of my hair and turned my head toward him. "I want to kiss those pretty little lips in private."

My heart raced, and I looked back at Jax, who ripped his lips away from the girl he was kissing. He took the cup that was in her hand and tipped it back to drink the entire contents. He stood and grabbed a different girl, pulled her against him, and kissed her.

I gasped as his hand went under her short skirt to cup her ass.

"Let's go." I stepped away, breaking my contact with Morgan.

He jogged to catch up as I walked toward the parking lot and slung an arm around my shoulder. "You know this doesn't change anything, right? We're just going to have a little fun."

I stopped as soon as we got to the top of the path and faced him. "Did you put fish in my dorm room?"

His eyes widened and his lips pulled at the

corners, fighting a smile. "You think I would do something like that?"

"Yes." I saw Ivy and Aiden walking up the path and grabbed his hand. "You can make it up to me. Where's the car?"

He took keys from his pocket and led me to Jax's black Maserati SUV. "I'm the designated driver tonight."

He opened the back door and I slid in with him hot on my heels. My ass was barely over into the next seat when he placed his hands on my cheeks and his lips were on mine.

What the hell was I doing?

I wrapped my fingers around his wrists, but instead of pulling away, I moved my head to a better angle and let his tongue in my mouth. It was as if I couldn't stop it once their mouths were on mine.

His hands ran down my arms and then he grabbed my waist and laid me out on the seat, settling between my legs. My body arched up to his as he moved his hips against mine. I gasped when I felt his erection against me.

I couldn't control my body's reaction to him.

"Shit, vixen, you taste and feel better than I could have ever imagined." He ran his thumb over my bottom lip.

"Why are you doing this?" My eyes searched his for answers.

"Because I'm horny and you're fine as fuck." He ran a finger along the edge of my shirt before dipping a finger under to touch the soft skin of my breast. "Have you let anyone kiss you here?"

My eyes grew heavy and my body wanted to arch into his touch. I never realized how much I craved a man's touch and mouth until then. It was like they'd opened up a floodgate of hormones that had been locked away.

He kissed down my neck to the exposed skin of my chest. I speared my fingers through his short brown hair.

"Treating me like crap... why?" I couldn't even formulate questions correctly. His lips stopped and he pulled back.

"You didn't meet your deadline." He sat back on his heels and rubbed his hands up and down my thighs. "Are you even trying to contact him?"

I nodded and my eyes landed on the evident bulge in his pants. "Why is it so important for me to contact my father? Do your parents work for him or have investments in his business?"

His hands stilled and he lowered himself back

on top of me, gripping my chin between his thumb and forefinger. "My parents are dead."

"I'm sorry, I didn't-"

The door was wrenched open and Morgan yelped as he flew off me and hit the car next to us. Jax's pissed off glare greeted me.

"Stay here." He slammed the door and turned and punched a laughing Morgan in the face.

Aiden and Ivy opened the door on the side the two assholes weren't fighting on.

"Hurry!" Ivy grabbed my hand and I pulled away from her. "Hurry before he's done beating the shit out of Morgan!"

"Wait." I got to my knees on the seat and looked into the trunk area. "This is my one chance."

Morgan and Jax were still fighting, and with the tinted windows, they couldn't see me. I climbed over the backseat.

"Your one chance for what? Riley! What the fuck are you doing?" Ivy screamed in a whisper. "They aren't going to fight for that long!"

"Leave the door open and then run to Aiden's car and peel out of here like I'm with you." She shook her head and looked at me like I was crazy. "Please! This is my one chance to find out why they hate my dad so much."

"You were just supposed to turn them against each other! Mission accomplished." She gestured to the other side of the SUV.

"They might know where my mom is." I gripped the headrest. "I have to try."

"You're crazy! They're going to hurt you." She looked through the window just as Jax slammed Morgan into the car on the other side of us again.

"I'll be fine." I ducked down and pulled my phone out to make sure it was silent. "I'll text you when we get to their house and when I get home. I still have some Uber credit."

"Fine. It's your funeral."

I laid down on my side and then started to doubt my decision. What if they caught me? They already had a few screws loose. I didn't think they'd hurt me, but what if this pushed them over the edge?

I needed to find out why they needed to find my father so bad, especially now that I knew the connection between my mom, my father, and Jax's father. I didn't want to think about the possibility of my mom going missing because of my father, but it was the only explanation that made sense.

My lips felt almost numb, and I brought my fingers to them. They were slightly swollen and most of the lip gloss was gone. I couldn't believe I'd made out with both Jax and Morgan. It was addicting and made me feel alive. I just wished assholes weren't the ones making me feel that way.

I heard the screeching of tires and Jax cursing. It was hard not being able to see what was going on, but heavy breaths came from the open door and then laughing.

"Fuck!" Jax must have seen I wasn't in the car and then the door was slammed shut. "Let's fucking go before I kill you."

I could still hear them through the windows.

"What about Blake?" Morgan's voice grew louder as he walked around the back of the vehicle. I held my breath, hoping he wasn't about to open the back.

"Did you see him back there? Oh, wait. You didn't because you were distracted by that... by that..."

Both doors in the front opened at the same time and the vehicle moved as they got in.

"Now, now, don't go calling names. It was only fair since you had two tastes that I got one too." Morgan sucked in air through his teeth. "Fuck, man, you've come a long way since the days you punched like a girl."

"She's mine." His voice came out raw and unhinged. "Just drive. I'm done here."

"Jesus, you need to calm yourself down before you shift right here in the car." Morgan started the car and revved the engine. The music was turned up to some hard-hitting song that shook the back window and made my ears hurt.

Shift? Was that a word similar to tea and bet? I didn't speak teenager slang, despite being one.

The music cut off. "Did you touch her?"

"Put your seatbelt on." We started moving, and if I wasn't so scared of them seeing the light from my cell phone, I would have turned on GPS.

I heard the click of the seatbelt and then a sigh. "This is such a fucking mess."

"I agree. I hate that it's not safe to have parties at our place. There is nowhere to adequately fuck a girl at the cove. Even in here, some asshole would probably film it and post it all over the place."

Was that all I was going to be? A fuck?

"She knows."

"What do you mean she knows?"

"She texted me last night and told me she knows our secret."

I heard the sound of air coming in and I

wrapped my arms around myself. It was way too cool out to have the windows open.

"That could mean anything." Morgan sounded worried. "There's no way she's ever seen us."

"It would explain the siren's knife."

My eyes widened. My mom's knife I had pulled on Jax had stolen his attention. He'd asked where I'd gotten it, but I hadn't thought twice about it.

"You were probably just seeing things. They were all destroyed by our people. Your dad said he remembers how big a deal it was from when he was a kid."

"What if they missed one, or one of them escaped?"

They both fell quiet and didn't turn the music back on. I was pretty sure I was far enough back that they couldn't hear me breathing to calm myself down.

I needed to hide the knife when I got home because if they were worried about me having it, they might try to steal it. If it was that important, I needed to protect it.

The car came to a stop and then pulled forward into a garage.

"If she really does know though..." Morgan turned off the engine. "What are we going to do?"

"We'll have to tell the admiral." Jax's voice sounded forlorn. "I fucking hate her, but..."

"But you don't want to see her get hurt... physically." Morgan laughed. "He said to do whatever it takes."

"I know. Seeing my sister this morning was a good reminder of what her father has done." The doors opened. "I need to swim."

The doors shut and the lights turned off, leaving me in the dark garage to wonder what his sister had to do with anything.

Chapter Ten

RILEY

I slipped out of the car and sent a text to Ivy. I understood that she was concerned about me, but she didn't need to be. I was trying to find answers, but so far I was more confused than ever.

Were they part of some kind of mafia organization? I was starting to wonder if it was possible after what I overheard. I shivered at the thought.

I turned on my phone's flashlight and looked around the garage. It was more square feet than the first floor of my townhouse and had off-roading vehicles, a boat, and two motorcycles. Lined on a shelf were different motorcycle helmets. I spotted Morgan's motorcycle and figured we must be at his house.

I slipped off my shoes and put them behind what looked like a trash can and tried the door. It opened and I took a deep breath before slipping in, hoping there weren't cameras.

I was in a hallway that led to a large living space. I stayed as close to the wall as possible and peeked around the corner. The house was gigantic.

Everything was sleek, modern, and clean. The entire back wall was glass, looking out onto a giant swimming pool. Surrounding the outdoor area was a railing, and then the ocean stretched as far as my eyes could see.

I hunched down and tiptoed into the room, hiding by the kitchen island. The kitchen was all white and smelled of lemons. There wasn't a crumb on the floor or counter. The stainless-steel appliances had not one fingerprint of grease splatter.

I peeked over the counter. They were in the pool, swimming laps. They must have gone straight outside and jumped in. The lights in the pool made the water look like it was the ocean.

I eyed the stairs and then dashed up them. I stopped at the top and listened to make sure they hadn't seen me. There wasn't a sound.

The first door on the right was cracked open, so I peered inside and pushed the door open the rest of the way. The room was a mess, and I could tell from the helmets and motorcycle posters that it was Morgan's room. I wondered who he lived with since his parents were deceased.

I didn't know what I was looking for, so I started with the desk, which was just as messy as the floor. I wasn't the neatest person in the world, but his room took it to a whole new level. I moved some papers around and only spotted notes. The desk drawers had a lot of junk and papers crammed inside.

I looked at the nightstand on the side of the bed he slept on. I only knew because he left it unmade. I stepped over a pile of clothes and pulled out the top drawer. Did he really need that big a box of condoms? I shook my head and opened the next drawer.

He had eye masks, a ball gag, wrist cuffs, and a switch in the drawer. I shuddered and closed the drawer. I might have been a virgin, but I was a well-read and knowledgeable one.

In the nightstand on the other side of the bed there was a roll of money that was all hundreds. It was tempting to take a few, but my conscience wouldn't allow it.

I left his room and shut the door the way it had been. The door across from his was open all the way. I walked in to a much more organized room. The bed was made and only a few shirts lay on the back of the desk chair. One of the walls was plastered with prominent black sports stars, and another with a giant canvas painting of sea life.

I ran my thumb over Jax's name signed on the bottom. I had no clue he was a painter or so talented. The painting looked like it was a photograph instead of done by hand.

I went to the desk where books were stacked neatly. There was a small container holding sticky notes and sticky flags and a cup with pens and highlighters.

I opened a drawer and pulled out a folder that looked jam packed with papers. Inside were printouts of college admission criteria. There were color coded highlights on each page. I flipped through them and spotted an opened Salinity Cove High envelope addressed to Blake.

Did Morgan and Blake live together? I wracked my brain, trying to remember if I'd ever actually seen any of their families. I hadn't been paying enough attention to them in the past to recall.

I knew exactly what it was by the seal broken on the back. Curiosity got the best of me and I pulled out his transcript. He had straight As and was ranked in the top ten percent.

I put it back inside the envelope and folder. Blake didn't act like a top student in class, but that didn't mean he wasn't one. The rumors about him paying people to do his assignments was still likely.

After his room turned up nothing, I tried the rest of the rooms. One was a guest room and another was locked. The last room was behind two double doors at the end of the hall.

I knew as soon as I cracked the door open that it didn't belong to anyone's parents. Jax's scent hit my nose, and in the corner of the room was an easel with a drop cloth laid underneath.

They all lived in this house without their parents? I thought that only happened in movies, but I guess when you're rich anything is possible. They were all eighteen as far as I knew, but leaving three guys to their own devices seemed negligent.

My eyes took in the master suite, which was way too luxurious for an eighteen-year-old still in high school. Like downstairs, the entire wall of the room was windows with a small terrace that looked out at the ocean.

I shut the door and stepped farther into the room, turning toward the bathroom that was encased in glass. The shower was against the glass wall, looking out to the ocean, and there was a giant tub right next to it.

Voices came from outside in the hall, and I looked around frantically for a place to hide. Where the hell was the closet door?

I heard a door shut down the hall and cursed under my breath. I ran to the other side of the bed and dropped to the floor right as the bedroom door opened. I saw his bare feet as he walked to the bathroom.

I needed to wait until the opportune moment and hightail it out of there. It was a completely stupid idea to hide in the back of the SUV and then come inside and snoop. I'd clearly lost my mind and my common sense over the past week. If I got caught they might call the cops, and then what? I had no one to bail me out.

The shower turned on and I scooted forward to peek around the end of the bed. My lips parted as Jax's bare, muscular ass greeted me as he stepped in the shower. He stood under the spray of water, facing away from me.

I prepared to dart around the bed and to the door. Even if he heard me, I should be able to get out of the room and house before he could catch up. It was doubtful he'd run after me naked. If he did, I didn't know if I would be able to not look.

I put a hand over my mouth to cover a giggle that threatened to bubble out of me at the image of his dick bouncing around as he chased me.

He turned to face the window, looking out to the ocean. His eyes were shut and his jaw hardened as he put his forearm against the window and put his forehead on it. He grabbed his cock and began stroking it, the water still hitting him from the side. He stroked himself from root to tip and stopped at the end of every pull to run his fingers around the crown and over the tip.

I was glued to my spot on the floor and my stomach clenched with need. His pace increased and the muscles in his arm flexed as he worked himself.

I needed to get out of there.

I scrambled on my hands and knees, and when I was just about to the door, my phone fell from my back pocket. It wasn't loud, but the second I looked back at the bathroom, Jax's eyes met mine over his shoulder.

His mouth opened and he threw his head back, ropes of cum shooting out onto the glass window in front of him.

I jumped up and tried to grab my phone, but it was too far back and Jax was already out of the shower.

I threw open the door and ran down the hall. I took the stairs as quickly as possible and turned the corner then came to a stop. Blake was coming in the door from the garage and looked right at me.

"What the-"

"Riley!" Jax's voice came from the top of the stairs as I ran through the kitchen to the other side of the house. "Get the fuck back here!"

I was in such deep shit. It would be a miracle if I made it out of the house without them catching me. And then what? I had no shoes and no phone. I'd be walking for hours to get home. It was what I deserved for being so stupid.

I made it through the living room and down another short hall which had a bathroom and an elevator button. I pressed it and it slid open immediately. There was no other choice. The bathroom was in the middle of the house and wouldn't have a window for me to escape out of.

I ran in and frantically pressed the button just as Blake rounded the corner and sprinted toward me. It slid closed just before he could reach me and began its descent.

"Fuck. Fuck. Fuck!" I was an idiot jumping into an elevator.

I had never seen their house from the outside, so I didn't know what the hell was going to be at the bottom. It stopped after what felt like five or six stories and I rushed out.

My eyes went wide and I turned to go back into the elevator, but the doors already slid shut. I pounded my fists on the metal, but I could already hear it moving.

I searched around frantically for a stairwell, but there was only the elevator. Talk about breaking fire code. I turned and looked at my surroundings.

I was in a cave that had lit up as soon as the elevator doors had opened. It was oddly quiet inside, but that wasn't what had scared me. The gently rippling water was what gave me pause. It was dark and looked deep.

There were two boats and three jet skis in the water. I didn't even know how they got out of the cave because there wasn't an exit. Against the rock face next to the elevator were storage cabinets.

I opened them but there was no space to hide. I looked back at the elevator and listened. The noise stopped and then it started moving again.

They were coming.

The only possible place to hide was one of the boats. I didn't know what else to do, so I ran down the platform and climbed onto one. I sat with my knees drawn to my chest in front of the driver's seat.

Maybe there was a way out that I wasn't seeing and they would think I swam out. I shuddered at the thought of having to find a way out of the cave through the water. I would just wait it out.

The elevator door dinged and I tried to calm myself down. My chest was heaving and I couldn't catch my breath. I curled into a tighter ball, trying to get my body to stop shaking.

"You check over there," Blake said.

I couldn't hear them searching and shut my eyes. The boat moved with the water and I bit down on the sleeve of my shirt, suddenly taken back to when I was seven.

My chest and throat burned as I coughed up water. My gasps for breath made me feel like I couldn't get enough air. I gripped the side of the buoy I was on as it rocked in the water and coughed so hard it felt like my throat was on fire.

I was going to die.

A head popped up and I rubbed at my eyes. Only his eyes and forehead were showing. His skin was as blue as the water and his eyes were amber and shaped like a cat's. My mouth

*opened to scream, but my vision tunneled and everything went
black.*

Someone grabbed my arm and yanked me to
my feet. I screamed and it echoed in the cave. Blake
had ahold of me and I twisted in his grip, shoving
at him.

I managed to slip out of his grasp, but he
reached for me again and our bodies collided. My
ankle rolled as I stepped on something inside the
boat and my balance was thrown off.

It happened in a split second. We hit the water
in a tangle of limbs with a scream leaving my lips.

He let go of me and I fought against the panic
that was threatening to render me helpless. I hadn't
been in the water since I was seven. I was able to
keep my head above water and I grabbed onto the
first thing I could.

A cry lodged in my throat and I tried to pull
myself up on the boat but every muscle in me was
shaking so I just held onto the rear platform of it for
dear life.

"Where's Riley?" Morgan asked.

"Help." My voice came out as a croak.

I heard a splash, and then faster than should
have been possible, Blake was wrapping his arms
around me. "Let go, Riley. I'll get you out of here."

"I can't."

He pried my fingers from the edge of the platform, and instead of putting me on the boat, he swam back around it to the ledge where Morgan was waiting.

He grabbed me and pulled me out of the water. Relief washed over me and my muscles went limp. They had been so tense that now they felt like jelly. A chill swept over me and I curled myself into a ball.

I heard them get into a small argument but wasn't really listening to them. The sound of my heartbeats in my ears was deafening. Blake scooped me into his arms, and the next thing I knew, he was setting me on the bathroom counter.

"You need to get out of these clothes. You're freezing." He started to pull the hem of my top away from my body.

I shook my head. I wasn't about to let them see me naked. I dug my nails into his arm and he looked at Jax, who had appeared in the doorway. I avoided looking at him after seeing him get off in the shower.

"We should be throwing her ass outside the gates, not coddling her." Despite Jax's words, he walked to the shower and turned on the water.

"Let's get her warm so she doesn't get hypothermia and then we can figure out how we want to deal with her."

I had almost forgotten why I was at their house in the first place. A shudder rocked through me as Blake stepped into the shower with me in his arms. He said something to me then dropped my legs. I sagged against him, clinging to his body.

"Come on, Riley. Stop being difficult."

Jax moved to my other side and gripped my arm. My body warmed with his touch, more so than from the warm water.

The water was shut off and I was handed to Morgan, who was waiting with a towel. I nodded when he said something and they shut the bathroom door as they left me.

Chapter Eleven

RILEY

*G*et it together, Ri.

I looked at myself in the mirror and frowned at the state I was in. I looked like something the cat dragged in. My brown hair was a curly mess and the eyeliner and mascara I had worn was melting off my face.

I used the edge of the towel and wiped my face off the rest of the way. My skin was blotchy from crying and my green eyes were wide and scared.

His eyes.

I shook my head and knew I was just projecting my memories onto the whole situation. As soon as I had hit the water, I was taken back to the sheer terror I had felt being pulled out to sea by a rip current.

It had been ten years since what the news had called a miracle. It wasn't a miracle. I still was convinced a sea creature that looked human had saved me. But even then, I knew no one would believe me.

Feeling a little more alive, I stripped out of my wet clothes and pulled on the pair of sweatpants and t-shirt Morgan had left for me. This whole night had been one giant mistake, but for some reason, when I was around the three of them, I threw caution to the wind.

Maybe it was my survival instincts kicking in, or I was just a glutton for punishment.

I towel-dried my hair and left my pile of wet clothes on the counter. It was time to face the music. The cops might even be waiting for me right outside to take me away in cuffs.

I opened the door and Morgan pushed away from the wall he was leaning against. "Blake went to change."

I stood in the doorway, not sure what to do. He stared at me without much of an expression on his face.

He pushed past me and grabbed the towel and stack of clothes. "I'll get these in the dryer. Why don't you sit?"

I followed him and stopped in the middle of their large living room. Now that I wasn't rushing around playing Harriet the Spy, the opulence of the room left me breathless.

The ceilings were about twenty feet high with a large glistening chandelier hanging from the center. The crystals were in just about every shade of blue, and it looked like ocean waves as the light filtered through them.

In the center of the room was a large white sectional that was covered in fluffy blue throw pillows. It was unexpected to see such a white sofa with a bunch of teenage boys. It probably had some protective finish on it to keep it looking clean.

I sat down at the end of the couch and brought my feet up. I was still chilled and took a blue throw off the back of the couch, wrapping it around me. The room was comfortable but wasn't my taste. It was too cold and reminded me of the ocean a little too much.

Blake came down the stairs and walked into the kitchen, his bare muscular chest on full display over the center island. He opened a cupboard, pulled out a mug, and put water into it. He put it in the microwave and watched me in the reflection of the door until the timer beeped.

"Do you want hot chocolate or tea?" He pulled the mug out and brought it to the island.

"Tea, please." I hugged a pillow to my chest and couldn't help but smell it. It smelled like the ocean. "Your house is nice. Where are your parents?"

He walked around the island and handed me the mug before sitting down near my feet. "Just us three live here."

"Alone?" I sipped the hot liquid and my insides heated. "That's a little odd."

I watched him over the rim of the mug. His brown skin was almost glowing with a bronze undertone and his dark nipples were hard. I thought about how he would react if I leaned forward and nipped one.

"You live alone right now, don't you?" I don't know if he unconsciously did it, but he put a hand on my feet and squeezed them.

"I'm not sure." I looked into my tea. Everything was so fucked and I didn't know what I was going to do.

There had to be a good explanation for where my mom was. I needed to search through her things again to see if I could find answers. Especially now that the Tritons were talking about a siren knife, and I knew for certain my mom had dated Jax's father.

"Maybe she ran off with your dad."

The thought had crossed my mind a time or two, but from all I knew, she despised the man. It wouldn't make sense for her to run off with a man she hated when she had a daughter she loved. "I don't think so. He left when I was a baby and anytime I ask about him, she shuts down."

Blake leaned forward and grabbed the remote off the coffee table. "Don't be shocked if Jax throws you to the curb when he gets back down here."

"He's not going to do anything." Morgan was back and stopped in front of me, frowning down at Blake. "What do you think you're doing?"

Blake waved the remote control in the air. "What does it look like I'm doing?"

Morgan leaned forward and took it from him. "Scoot over. If you get to sit next to her, so do I."

"I'm confused," I muttered as Blake and I moved over. One minute they were making my life miserable, and the next they were cuddling with me. The worst part was, I was letting them.

Maybe it was time to go to the doctor and have my head checked.

"What are you confused about? I thought you

were top ten in our class." Morgan plopped down next to me and pulled me back into the crook of his arm, almost causing me to spill my tea. "I guess those kinds of smarts don't extend to other areas."

"What's that supposed to mean?" I turned to look at him and he shrugged.

"You're the one that somehow broke into our house, got caught, then freaked out on us."

"Lay off it, Mo." Blake moved his hands under the blanket and began messaging the arch of my foot. "She's recovering."

He snorted. "Well, if this is how much recovery she needs after that level of physical activity, she'll never survive fucking one of us." He turned on the TV. "Or all of us."

I spit my tea back into my cup and the chill was suddenly completely gone. "I would never sleep with any of you, you're all just-"

"What is she still doing here?" Jax was standing at the side of the couch and glared down at me. "If she's well enough to run her mouth, she's well enough to be out on her ass."

"Don't be a douche canoe." Morgan flipped through the listings and put on a movie. "I love this movie."

I looked away from Jax and couldn't stop the laugh that came out. "*Finding Nemo?*"

"Don't judge."

Jax sat on the coffee table in front of us and took the tea out of my hands. "How did you get in our house and why?"

I looked down at my hands. Every time I looked at him now, I was going to remember how his back and ass muscles flexed as he came. Not to mention how his face looked.

"Look at me when I'm talking to you." His words were clipped and laced in annoyance. "We should call the police."

I met his stare and shifted in my seat, my body heating to a whole new level. "You broke into my house first."

Two wrongs didn't make a right, but it sounded like a good enough reason.

"Your back door was unlocked and you knew I was there." He ran a hand over his short hair that was cut close to his scalp. "You were hiding in my room, watching me as I jacked off."

"What?" Both Morgan and Blake sounded like prepubescent boys as their voices rose an octave.

I brought the edge of the blanket over my head before it was pulled down by Jax leaning forward.

"Don't play shy. You watched me as I came. How does it feel knowing I got off on catching you sneak out of my bedroom?"

I tried to move and Blake clamped an arm on my legs while Morgan grabbed my shoulder and held me there.

My embarrassment was through the roof and I thought what had happened with the jam on my car had been embarrassing. "I want it to stop."

"You know what you have to do then. Provoking us is only making your situation worse. Now, how did you get in here?"

"In the back of the SUV."

"Fuck." Morgan stood and glared down at me. "It was all a ruse?"

I could have tried to explain what happened, but I didn't feel I needed to. It didn't matter how I got in, the fact was, I did.

Hurt flashed across his face and he threw the remote in my lap and stormed off. I felt a second of guilt before I reminded myself that they were trying to make my life hell.

"I'll take you home." Jax stood and pulled my cell phone from his pocket. "You should probably put a passcode on this."

My eyes widened and I stood to follow him, but

Blake looped an arm around my waist and I fell into his lap. "We can take her home in the morning."

My pulse quickened. His hand was splayed on my stomach and I felt the heat of it through the shirt. I didn't realize I was sitting with my ass directly on his dick until it twitched against me.

"She'll go now." Jax came back to the couch and pulled me up by the hand.

I stumbled into his chest, my hands going to his bare pecs. I looked up at him and he put his hands on my shoulders, moving me away from him.

"Fine. You take her home when you're done playing with her." He stormed off just as Morgan had.

"Do you want me to take you home?" He looked between me and the television screen. "Or..."

If I went home, I'd have to deal with an empty house after having a traumatic night. Even if I spent the night on their couch, it was better to sleep in a blood thirsty school of sharks than the dark depths of my fears.

I sat down and pulled the blanket back around me. "I want to stay."

I WOKE feeling like I was back under the water again. An arm wrapped around my waist was holding me down. I whimpered and looked around frantically.

There was water everywhere.

"Hey. You're okay. I'm right here." The arm moved from around my waist and I was on my back looking up at Blake.

His hand came to my cheek and I released the breath I was holding. I blinked back the tears that threatened to fall and he brushed my hair back off my sweaty forehead.

"You're a mess, Kline." He chuckled. "It's barely three and you've had two nightmares."

I looked past him at the ceiling and walls. "Why does it look like we're underwater?"

"It's a projector. It's soothing. Well, for me anyway." He scooted to the edge of the bed and pressed a button, turning it off. "That better?"

He propped himself on his elbow next to me and stared.

"Yes. Why am I in your bed?"

"That couch isn't comfortable to sleep on." He brought his hand back to my hair again. "Plus, I wanted to piss Mo and Jax off by bringing you to my bed."

I turned onto my side to face him. "Don't you have a guest bedroom?" His hand moved back to my cheek and he gently moved his thumb across my skin.

"We do." I could see his dilated eyes in the faint light filtering in from under the door.

"Then why am I in here?" I brought my hand up to cover his and stopped him from moving it.

"It was an impulse decision. You should understand that." He moved closer and I rolled onto my back. "It's like you're a beacon drawing us to you."

His forearms went to the sides of my head and he moved a thigh over mine. I trembled as he stared down at me.

"I don't understand this." I looked down at his plump lips, the desire to feel them too strong to resist.

I brought my hand up and ran my index finger over the bottom one. He made a growling noise in his throat and his eyes darkened further.

"Did you kiss Morgan too?" I didn't know why he cared who I kissed, but I nodded. "Then it's only fair I get to kiss you."

"I-" His lips moved to my cheek and I lost my train of thought.

He rolled off me and onto his back, staring up at the ceiling. "I'm not like those two assholes though. I won't take advantage of you."

"I want you to kiss me." It felt painful to have him reject me, more than finding fish in my dorm or all the other crap they'd already pulled.

"You don't know what you want, Riley." He sighed and rolled away from me. "You shouldn't kiss or do anything else with guys who are complete assholes to you."

He was absolutely right, but I still wanted to kiss him.

Chapter Twelve

*R*iley made no sense to me. One second I was seriously entertaining the idea that she had siren in her ancestry, and the next, she was freaking out over falling in the water. As I watched her sleep, I couldn't figure her out.

I had wanted to kiss those pouty lips of hers so bad, but knew if she did have siren blood, that I had to tread carefully. I saw how the other two reacted to her when she was near. It was like watching two love-sick puppies.

Two love-sick puppies who were tormented by what we were doing to her. We couldn't defy an order from Jax's father, though. He was an admiral, and someday Jax would take his place with us at his side.

I sat at the edge of the bed and turned back to look at her. She slept peacefully now after her nightmares. Her hair fanned across the pillow in thick brown waves. It was getting harder for me to ignore the fact that I was attracted to her.

Sirens were supposed to be extinct. It was possible a few had escaped and found a life on land, but they would have been easy to detect. Sirens were lunatics, and once they knew they had power over men, they used it to excess.

Poseidon had managed to control them by gifting them knives that calmed their urges. He also gave them free rein to do whatever they wanted to men who didn't have the best intentions at sea.

I stood and stretched before grabbing a pair of sweatpants and my phone. I slipped out of the room, shutting the door softly behind me just as Morgan was coming out of his bedroom.

Our internal clocks were nothing if not accurate. We woke at six o'clock every day, not a minute earlier or later.

We walked down the stairs shoulder to shoulder and then he shoved me against the refrigerator. "Did you-"

"Even if I did, I'm not like you and go around bragging about it." I pushed him off me just as Jax walked into the room. "What does it matter? Both of you have already made out with her."

"You kissed her?" Jax put his hands on the edge of the island and glared. "I told you, she's mine."

I ignored him and pulled ingredients out of the refrigerator to make breakfast as Morgan started making coffee. "Have you two considered that it's possible your attraction to her isn't normal? That maybe she's causing it?"

Morgan made a disgruntled sound and got a mug out of the cupboard. "We would have noticed her before if she was what you are insinuating."

"Not necessarily." Jax sat on a barstool. "We'd never talked to her or been around her enough. She doesn't sing, does she?"

"Maybe we should ask her." I started mixing dough for biscuits. "I don't think the secret she thinks she knows is the one we fear."

If she did know about what we were, we'd have to contact the admiral about how to proceed. Humans weren't allowed to know about our existence. There were a few exceptions, but they had to be approved by the admirals.

"The last thing we need is for her to sing and put us under a spell." Morgan took a drink of his coffee. "There is something about her though…

maybe it's the fact that she's sexy as fuck and smart too. She also has that whole damsel in distress thing going on, which means she'd be just my type in the bedroom."

"She's only a damsel because of us." Jax stood. "When we find that fucker of a father of hers, I'm going to gut him from dick to throat and let Bubba feast on his intestines."

I put the biscuits I had just cut onto a tray and put them in the oven. "You would feed Bubba spoiled meat?" I laughed at the thought of the shark turning his nose up. "He'd hate you for feeding him such low-grade meat."

"You have a point." Jax sat down on the couch and turned on the news.

Morgan and I frowned at each other. Jax tortured himself on a daily basis by watching the round the clock coverage of the oil disaster. It was like he wanted to feel the pain every day to remind himself what our mission was.

Find Robert Kline and deliver him to the admiral.

It hadn't seemed that difficult when he'd assigned the task to us, but now it seemed impossible. Riley was either telling the truth or was motivated in some way to keep his location a secret.

In our world, fathers didn't leave their children. It was different with humans, but Riley's mom had never held a job. The money was coming from someone to pay for their townhouse that was walking distance from the beach, her and Riley's cars, and their lifestyle.

We'd done our research. Riley's mother, Natalia, was getting money from Robert. She had to be.

Morgan leaned against the counter as I cracked eggs in a bowl. "Do you think her mom really went on vacation?"

"No." I dug in the drawer for the whisk. "It doesn't make sense for her to run, unless she ran with Robert."

"Do you think Riley's considered that?" Morgan frowned into his coffee. "She's smart. She has to wonder."

"I think she only sees what she wants to see." I flipped the bacon and then poured the eggs in another pan. "Just like all humans."

I just wished she'd see that we weren't going to stop until we got what we wanted.

Chapter Thirteen

RILEY

I woke up to an empty bed. I slid my hands over the sheets to find them cold. Last night was out of character for me. I never did anything to get myself in trouble or have others look at me with anything less than respect.

Now, I was in bed with the enemy.

I checked my phone for messages to find none. In two days, my mom should be home, and if she wasn't... I tried not to think of it.

I slid out of bed and went to the bathroom before wandering into the hall. I could hear the television downstairs and hushed voices. The smell of food made my stomach grumble, and I took a calm breath and went to face the music.

Last night they were too nice to me since I had scared myself half to death. Today, I probably wouldn't be so lucky.

"We have to tell him-" Blake's voice cut off abruptly when I got to the bottom of the stairs. "Good morning."

I gave him a small smile and approached with caution. Blake was cooking at the stove, Morgan was sipping coffee, and Jax was sitting on the couch.

"You eat meat, right?" He flipped bacon and didn't flinch as it popped.

"Yes." I stood next to the island. "You know you can cook bacon in the oven and it won't pop you? If you line the baking sheet with foil, it's super easy to clean up."

Blake looked over his shoulder at me. "It doesn't taste the same."

"Do you want coffee?" Morgan took another drink. "I make a mean cup of espresso if you're into that."

"No, thanks." I looked over my shoulder at Jax who was glued to the television and I could see why. It was about the oil spill.

Out of the three of them, Jax was the most confusing. They all had a bad side to them, but Jax was the worst and was the most at odds with it. He had bigger mood swings than a pregnant woman.

I moved to the couch and sat down a seat away from him. He was in a pair of basketball shorts, similar to the pair he had on the night before, and no shirt. Even sitting he didn't seem to have an ounce of fat on him.

None of them appeared to have any body hair either, besides the hair on their heads. Jax and Blake both wore theirs shaved close to their scalps, while Morgan kept his short on the sides and longer on top.

"As you can see behind me, efforts are underway to save a pod of dolphins that swam through an uncontained patch of oil. Great progress has been made containing and eliminating the patches, but with such a wide area being affected, there are bound to be scenes just like this for months and possibly years to come."

The image cut from the reporter standing in front of a facility, to a group of men and women in the water with a pod of dolphins. The dolphins' eyes looked pained as they were cared for by the rescue workers.

Jax sniffled a few times and I peeked over at

him. Tears ran down his face. My heart clenched and I scooted next to him, taking his hand in mine. There was a fifty-fifty chance he'd react negatively.

"Your father did this." His voice was flat and I gulped the sudden emotion that welled up inside my throat. "He knew it wasn't safe to put an oil platform in that location and did it anyway. He went against protestors and used his money to get past the red tape."

I put my head against his shoulder and watched as the news showed oil being burned on the surface of the water. They were trying multiple ways to get rid of the oil, but with constantly moving water, the weather, and the sheer volume of the oil spill, it was difficult.

"I don't know my father." I whispered. "He hasn't responded to my emails or my calls. I don't know what else you want me to do."

"Try harder." He let go of my hand and stood, the switch being flipped and the glare back. He swiped at his cheeks. "I'm taking you home."

"Let's eat breakfast first." Morgan gave Jax a warning look.

Jax sat back down as I stood, crossing his arms. "I've suddenly lost my appetite."

"Awesome. More for us." Blake set a tray on the

dining room table that was right next to the floor to ceiling windows. "Let's eat."

I looked down at Jax and then went and sat at the table. Blake had made scrambled eggs, bacon, biscuits, and cut fruit.

"This is a nice spread." I served myself and looked out the big windows that look out to the ocean. "Aren't you scared the cliff might collapse?"

Morgan snorted and bit into a biscuit. A few crumbs were still on his chin, and I wanted to lean over and brush them off. There was an odd compulsion to touch them and let them touch me when I was near them. It was like I was possessed.

"It's reinforced with steel. This baby isn't going anywhere in the next century." Morgan pointed his fork at me. "And all the windows have storm shutters."

I had so many questions. Once I finished chewing, I decided to ask since they were being pleasant. "Where are your parents?"

They looked at each other and Blake answered for them both. "They work for the same corporation, Trident Industries. Our great, great grandparents founded this town."

I'd heard the name thrown around, but never

paid much mind to what they did. It seemed every-thing with these three had to do with tridents. Even our school mascot, a shark, held a trident.

"But you haven't lived here all your life, have you?" I wracked my brain trying to remember them from elementary and middle school. There were two of each which filtered into the only high school. "You must have gone to North Cove Elementary."

"We were homeschooled." Jax pulled the chair out at the end of the table and Blake slid him the tray of food to make his plate. "We're too advanced to deal with elementary and junior high bullshit."

I tensed as he stared at me. Morgan chuckled. "He doesn't bite... unless you ask him nicely."

My face flamed and I busied myself eating instead of talking. The food was good and I wondered what else Blake could cook, and if the other two could as well.

Blake cleared his throat. "I'll take you home once you're finished. Morgan dried your clothes."

"Or you can just take those and give them back to me at school." Morgan put his napkin and fork on his plate. "If you want."

"I'll take her home." Jax had only eaten half his food but stood. "Let's go."

Blake and Morgan made no protest. Jax was definitely the leader of their trio.

I followed him and he handed me a paper bag with my clothes in it. "My shoes are in your garage."

"Of course they are." I followed him out to his car and he opened the back. "You'll sit back here."

"What?" I was still strapping my sandals on as he got in the driver's seat.

I heard the locks click and went to the passenger side, trying to open it. He opened the garage door and then looked at me. "Get in the back."

My eyes stung for a moment, but I complied and climbed in, the door shutting me into the back area. Instead of laying this time, I looked over the seat at him.

"Why are you such a moody ass?" I put the bag of clothes on the seat in front of me and his eyes went to it as he pulled out of the garage.

Their house was fairly large and modern looking. It was a bigger property than I expected. We stopped at a gate and waited for it to slide open.

I hitched a leg over the back of the seat, ready to climb into an actual seat.

"Don't even think about climbing over that seat or I'll make you walk home."

"Might be worth it." I muttered before sitting back down.

We were about ten minutes from the community of townhouses I lived in judging by what I saw out the window. Now I knew how he had gotten home so fast after being inside my house.

"Do you have the security guards and police in your pocket?"

"What is this, the mafia?" I could almost hear him roll his eyes.

"I don't know, is it?" I opened my phone and pressed record on the camera. "You're the one that got back here in under twenty minutes and then convinced the two officers that you were with a girl."

"You're a smart woman. Use your brain." He laughed. "Well, I thought you were a smart woman until you stowed away back there and snuck into our house."

"Morgan was making out with me on the backseat and my cellphone fell under the seat. I was just retrieving it. After you beat the shit out of him, I was too scared to say anything, so I just... went along for the ride."

"You were in my room."

"I had to go pee." I knew I could always cut this part out of the recording. "I panicked."

"You weren't panicked enough to not watch me jerk off thinking about you."

I was glad he couldn't see me because I was sure my face was beet red. "Why would you tell me that?"

"You want to know what I was thinking about?" I heard the sound of the blinker and knew we were pulling off the highway and into the area I lived.

"Not particularly." *Yes, please tell me.*

"I was thinking about that night you were in my dorm room and I had you right where I wanted you. How I would have eaten that sweet pussy of yours until you were screaming for me to give you an orgasm."

I gulped. "And?"

"I also imagined you taking my cock in your hand, just like I was, and letting me come all over those gorgeous tits of yours."

I shifted and squeezed my legs together. Why was I getting turned on by what he was saying? Bad, pussy, bad.

"I could have taken you for myself the other night, but you called the cops before even hearing me out." He made a tsking sound.

I was quiet and did a silent little victory dance in my head that he brought up the break in. I almost had him. "Why did you break into my house?"

The car came to a stop. "The same reason you broke into mine and were in my room."

"I already told you, I didn't break in." The back door swung up. "Thanks for the ride. I guess."

"Enjoy your weekend." He smiled. I was confused. His mood swings were giving me whiplash.

I jumped out of the back after turning off the recording and walked to the side gate. Aiden had my keys in his car and I hadn't even thought about texting him to bring them to me. I had a spare one hidden in the back.

The Maserati backed out of the driveway and it was then I realized the symbol on the front was a trident. They really had a thing for them.

I slipped into the backyard. I needed a hot shower and a giant glass of Sprite.

I lifted the cover to the burner on the barbecue grill and pulled out the spare key. I unlocked the back door and then came to a screeching halt.

No wonder he had oddly told me to have a nice weekend. There was sand everywhere.

CLEANING the sand had taken most of the day Saturday and part of the day on Sunday with the help of Aiden. There was nowhere they could have gotten in unless they had a key. I wouldn't be putting the spare key back outside again.

Sunday afternoon, the sand was gone, but my annoyance wasn't. I had put a message on the community app, asking if anyone had seen a vehicle delivering sand, but got no responses.

That much sand didn't end up in a house without being seen. There was now a pile big enough to make a sandcastle on the back patio. I had spent all the time I should have been searching for my mom ridding the entire downstairs of the pesky granules.

I stood at the door of my mom's room and looked around. She had left it almost too neat. I went to her dresser and looked in each of the drawers. I was glad she hadn't taken all of her clothes, otherwise I'd really be freaking out.

I lifted the mattress to see if anything was hidden between it and the base, but came up with nothing. I laid on the floor and looked under the bed. It was dusty and there were a few lost tissues and a stray hair tie, but nothing else.

I sat against the bed and hugged my knees to my chest. I could have just been blowing everything out of proportion. She was supposed to be back the following afternoon and would find it hilarious that I freaked out for no reason.

Getting to my knees, I opened the nightstand Ivy had looked in. The top drawer had a few romance novels, Antacid, and a flashlight. I flipped through the books and skimmed the dog-eared pages. They were passages about love and fighting for yourself.

I hesitated on opening the bottom drawer. Ivy had freaked out and slammed it shut. I really didn't need to see what was inside, but shut my eyes and pulled it open before I could talk myself out of it.

I cracked open an eye and then sighed in relief. The way Ivy had reacted, I thought there was a massive dildo in the drawer. Sure, there were two different toys, but nothing to be embarrassed about.

They were sitting higher in the drawer than they should have been. There was a hand towel spread out under them, so I pulled it back and shouted in excitement.

There was a plastic box under them. I pulled it out and sat on the bed with it in my lap. My mom was a smart woman hiding something under her sex toys.

I unclasped the sides of the box and pulled the lid off. There was a blue envelope with my name on it and that was it.

My birthday was in a few weeks. Maybe this was where she hid smaller presents and I had just uncovered her secret hiding place.

I opened the blue envelope and pulled out the card. It was just a folded piece of card stock. I opened it and inside was a letter to me.

Ri,

If you're reading this, that means something has happened to me to cause you to go snooping. When you're done reading this, you need to destroy it.

I can't put much in this letter, but know that I love you. Anything I do, it's for you, and you're going to have to trust that my decisions aren't from a place of self-ishness.

Over the years I've quietly been stashing away money for you. Just enough where your father wouldn't grow suspicious and come back into our lives. Hidden in one of your favorite things is a list of contacts.

Call the first number and tell him the situation. I love you.

Mom

I'd been right all along, something had happened to my mom.

Chapter Fourteen

RILEY

I'd found the list of numbers inside *Little House on The Prairie*. It had taken me almost an hour of flipping through books on my bookshelves to find the small piece of paper that had three numbers.

The man that answered hadn't said much and we arranged to meet on Tuesday after school.

It had been a week since my life had taken a drastic turn from sitting in the background to being the center of attention. It felt surreal that three teenagers could so easily flip the switch on someone's life.

I still wasn't sure what to do about the video I had recorded in the back of the car. I wasn't sure if it was incriminating enough, and it also incriminated me. If they wanted to turn the tables and say I broke into their house, I'd be in just as much trouble as Jax.

I parked my car and shut my eyes, trying to calm my nerves before facing the three assholes that were making my life hell.

A knock sounded on my window and I jumped. Morgan stood with the paper bag I had left on the back seat of Jax's car. I swung open my door, hitting him with it.

"Ow. What was that for, vixen? I thought we were friends now." He shoved the bag into my hands. "You forgot your clothes. Where are mine?"

"I burned them." I looked into the bag. "Where are my underwear and bra?"

"They're on the bottom." Morgan looked over the top of my car. "Gotta go."

He took off at a jog and at the gate, threw his arm around a girl's shoulder and kissed her temple. I couldn't see who she was from the back, but she had long, bleach blonde hair and shorts that almost showed her ass cheeks. Maybe I'd report her for violating the dress code.

I threw the bag into my car and slammed the door. It's not like he was mine, yet seeing him touch another woman made my blood boil.

I was losing it. Why was I jealous?

"Oh, shit. What happened?" Aiden fell into step with me as I walked toward the gate. "It can't be worse than sand."

"Thanks again for helping me." I looped my arm through his. "I never knew sand was so intrusive."

"We could have just left it and your mom would have a nice surprise waiting for her this afternoon. It could have been payback for not responding to your calls and for taking your money." We got to my locker and I shoved the stuff I didn't need until later into it.

"What if she isn't back when I get home?" My mom was supposed to be back in the early afternoon, but I had been brushing off the idea that she wouldn't be home. Now that I had read her letter, I was leaning more toward her not returning.

"The police said you have to wait twenty-four hours, yeah?" I nodded, and we walked toward English. "Then we deal with it when we get to that point."

"I have to go to the bathroom. I'll see you in class."

We separated and I went into the bathroom. I had needed a pick-me-up after my long weekend and drank coffee even though I didn't care for it. It made me jittery and have to pee way more than usual.

I stepped out of the stall and was washing my hands when I heard the lock and looked up.

Melissa.

With her were the two girls Jax had kissed from the bonfire and the girl who had made the fish breath comment the first day of school. The same girl Morgan had wrapped his arm around before school.

They stood blocking the door with looks on their faces that I thought were only reserved for bitches in mean girl movies.

"Can you please move?" I threw my paper towel in the trash and faced them. There was just the five of us in the bathroom, to my dismay.

"We need to talk." Morgan's plaything stepped forward and I took a step back toward a stall.

I knew the predicament I was in. I wasn't a fighter and there were four of them. I wasn't sure how much locking myself in a stall would help besides putting me closer to becoming a swirly victim.

"Talk?" I could make it into the stall I had just come out of, but wasn't sure I would be able to lock the door in enough time. My body would be able to hold the door shut.

"Morgan is mine. I want you to stay away from him."

"Not a problem. Are we done here?" I was inches from the stall when Melissa lunged forward and grabbed me by the ponytail.

She was strong and she slammed me against the section of wall between the stalls. "We aren't done."

I suppressed the urge to scream for help or fight back. I didn't need to make this worse on myself. "What else?"

"We have papers due in two weeks. You'll write them for us." Of course that was what Melissa wanted. She had to take summer school every year.

I couldn't do that. "We'll get caught." I flinched as Melissa grabbed shoulders and spun me around so my face was against the wall.

I attempted to free myself, but her nailed thumb pressed against the base of my skull. "How hard do you think I have to press to cause damage?" The other girls laughed.

"Let me go."

"Stay away from them." Melissa shoved me and my chin hit the wall, my teeth piercing my lip. "Ta-ta for now."

They were gone before I could even turn around. I spit the blood coming from my lip into the sink and held a paper towel to the split skin.

The bell rang and I groaned. In all my years, I had never gotten a tardy. The goody-two-shoes in me wanted to cry, but the new side of me was pissed and wanted blood.

An eye for an eye.

I walked out of the bathroom and almost ran into Officer Thomas. "You're late."

No shit, Sherlock. "Four girls jumped me in the bathroom." I moved the paper towel away from my lip and pointed. "What are you going to do about it?"

He had already started walking away and stopped, turning back to me with a scowl. "I don't like your attitude."

I don't like your face. "My apologies. I thought your job was to serve and protect."

"Get to class." He turned and walked off.

How much were the Tritons paying him to ignore me? Instead of heading to class, which I was late to already, I went straight to the office.

"Excuse me. Is Mrs. Miller in?"

The secretary looked up from her computer and her eyes widened. I knew my hair was half falling out of the ponytail and there were a few drops of blood on my shirt.

"Don't you mean Mrs. Angela, the nurse? Mrs. Miller took a leave of absence. We aren't sure when she'll return."

My stomach dropped. "What do you mean she took a leave of absence? I just saw her on Friday!" My voice cracked. "She didn't say anything about leaving and said I could come to her anytime."

"Sometimes life happens. Let's get you into the nurse's office."

I was freaking out. Instead of listening to her or asking to see the principal, I walked to English on a mission. Maybe if other people saw what they had done to me, they would be on my side.

I threw the bloody paper towel in a garbage can and pulled open the door to English with a flourish. Every single head turned my direction.

Mrs. Williams stood from her desk. "Riley, what the hell happened?"

I ignored her question and the fact that I looked bad enough to cause her to have a slip of the tongue. I marched right toward Blake, who stood.

He opened his mouth to say something and I smacked him across the face. His face turned with the slap and gasps spread across the room. Blake's eyes flared and his jaw clenched as he turned his face back to look me in the eye.

"Keep your pussies of the week away from me." I turned and left the room.

I THOUGHT my breaking point would be a little further down the line, but apparently not. I hid out in the bathroom, worrying about whether I was going to be suspended. Yet another thing that hadn't even been in the realm of possibility a week ago.

The bell rang, signaling the end of first period. I had cleaned myself up and besides the slight swell on my bottom lip and the fury in my eyes, I looked like myself again and not a deranged lunatic.

I checked my phone and had texts from not only Aiden and Ivy, but the entire lunch crew and a number I wasn't familiar with.

Unknown: Who did that to you?

Me: Who is this?

Unknown: Blake. Where are you? I convinced Mrs. Williams not to write you up.

I shoved my phone back in my bag and left the

bathroom. Did he want recognition shouted from the rooftops? He knew damn well who did it to me.

I entered Psychology and sat down in my seat, pulling my notebook out and ignoring the stares and whispers that were being sent my way. Now I was going to be known as the crazy girl who smacked guys.

Hopefully no one got that on video.

The tension was just leaving my shoulders when Blake walked in and came to stand by my desk. "Outside."

I looked up at him and then at the teacher who was watching us like a hawk. Blake looked over at Mr. Bancroft and he gave Blake a nod.

"You're paying off the teachers now too? Unfuckingbelievable." I crossed my arms. "I'm not leaving this room. Go get fucked by your little bitches."

"Ms. Kline, need I remind you that you are in a classroom?" Mr. Bancroft didn't look up from his computer. "Sit down, Blake. She doesn't want to talk to you."

Blake slid into the seat in front of me, even though it wasn't his assigned spot.

The rest of the morning passed without much fanfare, but that didn't stop me from being on high alert. I gave up trying to hide and sat in the cafeteria with the only people who weren't giving me looks like I had ten heads.

Melissa and the other three girls who had cornered me in the bathroom were sitting at a table on the other side of the cafeteria away from the Tritons. It hadn't taken Blake long to figure out who had assaulted me in the bathroom. I should have been happy they hadn't sent them, but it didn't matter.

Their hatred toward me had extended to others now. I had a giant target on my back.

"Stop glaring at them." Aiden was picking at his food. "Maybe the principal or the police need to get involved. They did break into your house again."

I had taken pictures and videos of the sandstorm that looked like it had blown through the entire bottom floor of the house. They hadn't stepped foot upstairs from what I could tell.

"I think they did something to Mrs. Miller." I bit into a fry and inhaled sharply as the salt stung my busted lip. "And they're paying the resource officers to ignore things. They're probably paying the police chief."

Piper snorted. "You sound like a crazy person."

I dropped a fry and glared at her. "You try

having three assholes making your life a living hell and literally have no adults paying any mind."

"You could go to social media or the news." Ivy pushed her tray away. "We could beat their asses."

I snorted. "What good is the media going to do? They won't care about a kid being bullied."

I did have the video where Jax practically admitted to breaking and entering, but I had listened to it twice and there was no way to edit it without it sounding manipulated.

I was on my own on this one. I just needed to be prepared for things to get ugly.

Chapter Fifteen

MORGAN

*W*e were assholes. I normally didn't care what people thought about me, but for some reason, when that vixen with green eyes set her glare on me, I cared more than I should have.

"Are we really going to do this?" I crossed my arms over my chest and waited as Jax tied the bra and panties to the flag pole. "Seems a little... childish."

He glared at me in typical Jax fashion and pulled the rope to raise the American flag right along with red lace boy shorts and a red lace bra. God bless America and the need for sexy lingerie.

"It's necessary. We need to remind her that we

still need her father. Friday night and Saturday morning set us back a bit." He pulled a hundred out of his back pocket as we walked back onto campus, handing it to the head resource officer.

I never had liked Officer Thomas, but he was easily paid off and left us alone. The last thing we needed was a nosy police officer. Most could be bought as long as you weren't committing a murder. There were still quite a few that refused to acknowledge we had all the power. We let the admiral take care of them.

"Have you entertained the thought that maybe she is telling the truth about him?" Blake stopped as we got to the building his class was in. "She has nothing to gain from lying about it."

"Someone is paying for everything and it's definitely not that mom of hers." Jax glanced back at me. "What do you think?"

"I think we need to up the stakes to make sure." Honestly, I didn't know what to think about her claims that she didn't know her father.

Regardless of my thoughts on the matter, Admiral West was putting pressure on us. With the reach he had, he had already exhausted all sources of information on the whereabouts of Robert. Riley appeared to be the only way that might lead us to him.

I didn't bother going back to class and sat down on the planter ledge, waiting for school to be out. I was so over the high school experience. Swimming was about the only thing it had going for it.

And the girls. Always the girls.

The bell rang and a flurry of activity came out into the halls. We had someone post about "Riley taking to the pole" on social media.

Sure enough, students came racing to the flag pole to take pictures and laugh. Riley was nowhere to be seen, but it wouldn't be long. She'd have to walk right past it to get to her car.

Emily sauntered over to me, swaying her hips like she was the hottest thing on Earth. She wasn't, especially with her horrible dye job and shorts that let any guy practically see her cooch. She sat down on my lap and wrapped her arms around my neck.

"What do you want?"

"When are you going to stop being mad at us? We said we were sorry." She stuck out her bottom lip as if that would work on me. "You should be happy we roughed her up a little."

I removed her arms from around my neck. "We

didn't ask you to do our dirty work for us. Not to mention, we never asked anyone to rough her up."

She stood and put her hands on her hips. "You are so confusing!" She marched off with a flick of her blonde hair and I rolled my eyes.

I looked at the time on my watch. Any minute, Riley would be rounding the corner after stopping at her locker. She was going to be a force to be reckoned with during dance. It would piss her off further when she discovered I'd be there today.

As if on cue, she rounded the corner with Ivy and came to a stop, looking up at the flag pole. Instead of having a reaction, she walked straight to it, pulled the ropes to bring it down, and untied her panties and bra. She raised the flag to half-mast and then turned and gave me a look so deadly that I wondered if she hadn't put the flag half-mast as a threat.

My cock stirred in my pants.

She and Ivy ignored the laughter and phones recording them and went into the parking lot.

I followed a safe distance behind her to the dance studio, but instead of turning into the parking lot, she kept driving. She turned into a strip mall with a coffee shop and sat in her car for a few minutes before going in.

I got off my bike and followed her inside. She was already seated with her back to me, a middle-aged man across from her.

I slid into the seat behind her and hoped she wouldn't notice me.

Chapter Sixteen

RILEY

I was fuming as I left school on Tuesday. I hadn't even looked in the bag with my clothes in it, but I should have known they'd do something with my underwear. Everyone knew they were mine too thanks to social media.

Social media was fun until you were the subject of the entertainment.

I drove a little faster than I should have to the coffee place where I was meeting Mr. Nguyen, the trustee for whatever fund my mom had set up for me. He had wanted me to meet him at his office, but I wasn't going to a strange man's office.

Yet, I'd sneak into some strange boys' house. I was on the hot mess express and I needed to get off before I crashed.

I spotted the man easily. He was the only one dressed in a suit with a briefcase sitting on the table in front of him. I'd picked this location because it had high-backed booths that allowed for some privacy.

"Mr. Nguyen? I'm Riley." We shook hands and I slid into the seat across from him.

"Ms. Kline. Any word from your mother?" When I shook my head, his eyebrows pinched together and he removed his glasses. "She thought this might eventually happen."

I thought I'd be more upset or frantic that my mom was now overdue on her arrival time, but sometime over the past several days, a numbness had washed over me. It was like my brain couldn't process the fact that she might be in trouble.

"After I'm done here, I'm going to the police station to file a missing person's report. They said I had to wait twenty-four hours after she was supposed to return." I folded my hands on the table. "Is CPS going to put me in a foster home?"

"You're almost eighteen. Unless you are a danger to yourself or your living situation is a danger, you'll age out before they can even get anything in place." He pulled some papers out of a briefcase. "I'm sorry you're going through this. As soon as your mom had you, she began preparing in case this happened."

"Why would she need to prepare?" Everything was a big fat question mark, and I hated that I had no clue what was going on.

The man was silent for a few moments. "I am under strict guidelines to only give you certain information for your own protection. Not that I know much anyway. Now, do you have all of the unpaid and overdue notices?"

I handed over the papers I had brought with me. There had been an entire folder of unpaid bills in her files. She had stopped paying in June. "How long until they release some of the money?"

"I have some pull with the judge. A week tops. I don't foresee any difficulties in getting this taken care of. Your mom put it in a trust because she was scared a regular account would be too vulnerable." He slid an envelope across the table to me. I opened it and peeked inside, seeing a small stack of hundred-dollar bills. "In the meantime, here some money to cover your everyday expenses. Take care of the essentials first. Gas, electric, water, cell phone. Those will be the first things that get disconnected due to nonpayment."

I had no clue about what went into cost of

living every month, but I needed to learn quickly. "You can't tell me where you think my mom might be?" He had to have some clue where she might be if he wasn't shocked when I called him.

"Did she take the knife?" He folded his hands on top of his briefcase and looked around the coffee shop.

"No."

"Don't let anyone know about it." He lowered his voice. "It's been in your family for a long time and is one of a kind. If she left it for you, it means she's not safe."

"It's just a fancy knife. I don't understand how her leaving it-"

"That is what she told me to tell you." He sighed. "None of it made sense to me either, but she said it was better if I didn't know."

"Am *I* safe?"

"You told me you were being bullied?"

"Yes. They seem to have the administration and campus security on their side. The school counselor I was talking to mysteriously went on leave."

"What are the boys' names?" I told him and he took his glasses off again and ran a hand over his face. "You need to stay away from them."

"It's kind of hard when they keep coming at me." I bit my lip. "I feel... drawn to them."

"Your mother didn't say anything about them being at your school. You need to stay away from them. They come from a lot of power. Finn..." His eyes widened and he put his glasses back on. "I have to go. I've said too much. Just trust me. Stay away from them."

He left me with a sour feeling in my stomach and a lot for me to think about.

"YOU'VE BEEN STARING at that screen like that for the last half-hour." Tory waved a hand in front of me and I snapped out of my pity party.

I'd like to see anyone be able to concentrate after being assaulted and having your underwear flown for the world to see. And it was only Wednesday afternoon.

"Just a lot on my mind."

Ashley came to stand by my computer. "Riley, I need your forty dollars for food still."

"Our first stay-late isn't for another few weeks. I'll give it to you then." I didn't look up from the computer where I was now moving pictures from one folder to another instead of staring blankly at it.

"I need it to be able to plan. It's been the same every year. Do you not have the money or something?"

I glanced up at her and she smiled sweetly at me. She was becoming increasingly more of a bitch. She hadn't been half bad before this year. How quickly people change.

"I won't have it for a few weeks." I wasn't going to give her what little money I did have. That money was for important bills, food, and gas.

She rolled her eyes and moved up a row to Jax, who was working on a layout for the football section. He hadn't said a word to me all week.

"That layout looks great, Jax." Ashley put her hand on his shoulder and gave it a squeeze. "You know, if you ever need extra help with the design program, we can always arrange a time after school to work together."

He didn't look away from the screen, but he didn't shrug her hand off either. "Are you the layout editor?"

"No, but this is my fourth year." Her hand slid over the front of his shoulder, straight for his chest.

I cut a glance to Tory, who was watching the

show with wide eyes. I looked back in just enough time to see Jax grab her hand and I thought he was going to push her away, but instead, he pulled her into his lap.

Ashley glanced at me and smirked before wrapping her arms around Jax's neck. I gripped the mouse hard and resisted the urge to chuck it at them.

"Maybe you can help me." He put his mouth near her ear but was still talking loud enough for me and Tory to hear. "I'm not sure how to fit this in."

Ashley adjusted herself in his lap and took the mouse. He put his hand over the top of hers. "Well, to get it in you have to move it like this."

Tory snorted. The whole interaction was ridiculous, and I wondered if he was doing it to annoy me. If so, it was working.

"I tried pulling it to this side, but it wouldn't come."

I stood and Tory tried to grab my arm as I walked around the desk. I went and stood behind his monitor.

"Can I help you?" Jax moved his hand to Ashley's waist and dug his fingers into her shirt.

"This is a classroom, not a bar to pick up on girls."

"Stop being such a prude." Ashley put his hand on her thigh. "Jealousy isn't a good look for you, hon."

I yanked the cord from the back of the computer. I knew it was petty and childish, but I was fed up and honestly didn't care.

"What the fuck?" Jax stood, moving Ashley off him and causing her to stumble. He put his hands flat on the desk and leaned forward as far as he could. "You're going to pay for that."

"Mr. West. What is going on over there?" Mr. Garcia stood and crossed his arms.

"Nothing." He sat back down as I plugged his computer back in.

I went back to my computer and he pulled the program back up. The page he had been designing was blank. His hand tightened on the mouse.

"Remind me not to piss you off," Tory muttered. "I guess he'll learn to save his work now."

Or he'll learn not to mess with me.

MAYA NICOLE

I DIDN'T ENJOY STUDYING with others, and one of the reasons was because not everyone was focused on school. We were required to meet twice a month for study group for an hour *to build academic discord and develop supportive relationships.*

It was bad enough I was distracted by the vague warnings the lawyer had given me, but now my mind kept replaying the scene in yearbook. Maybe I shouldn't have unplugged his computer like I had. He had worked all period on the varsity spread and I had ruined it.

The quiet of the library gave my mind too much time to wander. When I was able to focus, someone would slam a book shut, a backpack would be unzipped, or Blake would make a noise.

I should have faked cramps and gone home instead of staying and wasting my time.

Blake tapped his pencil on his paper before making a noise and then writing frantically. Me, Aiden, and a girl named Trisha gave each other looks and went back to our assignments.

The sound of a ripping page filled the immediate area and our eyes snapped back to Blake again, who didn't seem to care that he was distracting us all. He folded the paper he had ripped out of his notebook and then grinned at us.

Were they purposely trying to get on my last nerve? I was hanging on by a thread and about to snap. I ignored his grin and read the passage I had started reading for what felt like the tenth time.

The paper he folded landed in front of me. I gave him an exasperated look and then wadded up the paper and threw it toward the trashcan, missing.

He frowned. "Why'd you do that?"

"We're supposed to be working on homework and keeping each other on task." I stood and picked up the paper. "Writing notes and composing a drum solo is not staying on task."

"Well, at least read it." He turned back to his binder.

Aiden and Trisha gave me curious glances but then both got back to work. I did the same without opening the note.

I felt his eyes on me as I tried to take notes and then he nudged my foot with his. He was insufferable.

I unfolded the paper and turned to face away from the group so they couldn't see my reaction.

Jesus Christ, he'd written me a sexy note.

I can't concentrate on anything with you sitting next to me. Every time you stick the tip of your pen against your lips, I can't stop where my brain goes. I want to be that pen. Let's sneak to the bathroom and I'll give you a little late afternoon snack.

My pulse sped up and I put the pen against my lip while I considered what to write back. I could tell him he was disgusting or to knock it off. But that was what he wanted.

I wrote a note back underneath his.

I want to show you just what I can do with this mouth and my pen. Then I want to reach my hand over and feel how hard I get you.

I handed it to him under the table and he smirked as he opened it and read it. His nostrils flared as he looked up at me.

I smiled and looked down at my assignment, bringing my pen back to my mouth. I rubbed it against my bottom lip before putting the end in my mouth and closing my lips around it.

He shifted in his seat and I looked up at him through my lashes. I moved the pen in and out of my mouth a few times before biting down on it hard enough to make a sound.

He grimaced and then started laughing.

Trish threw her pen on the table and closed her books. "This is useless. It's almost time to go anyways. Thank fuck we only have to do this every other week."

"That was really messed up, Riley." Blake packed his stuff. "I have swim practice anyway."

He left without a glance back, and Aiden started laughing. "What the hell was that about?"

"He wrote me a nasty note, so I responded that I would show him what I'd do."

"Oh, man." Trisha laughed. "I don't get how those guys are so popular and why so many follow them blindly."

"They are rich asshole athletes. That's a turn on for some, I guess." He gave me a pointed look. "They will only lead to a case of crabs and heartache."

"I think we should meet without him." Trisha and Aiden followed me out of the library. "We can just tell him we aren't going to meet two Wednes-days from now."

"I agree. Mrs. Williams should understand."

The last thing I needed was for my grades to slip too.

Chapter Seventeen

RILEY

My world was becoming a blur of school and trying to locate my mother. The police didn't seem to care that she was still missing. It didn't help that all the evidence pointed to her taking off. It was no use telling them it was out of character.

I rolled over in bed and stared at my alarm clock that was about to go off. I had been up most of the night listing payments that had to be made as soon as I got any money from the fund my mom had in my name.

I wanted to just stay in bed and wait for everything to be over, but she wouldn't want me to do that. I turned off the clock before it went off and went into the bathroom to take a shower.

I looked in the mirror and frowned at my reflection. I barely recognized myself, even though I looked the same. My hair had certainly seen better days, but nothing else had changed.

The change had come from inside and I saw it in the way my shoulders pulled forward slightly and the frown that was etched on my face. Even my eyes looked sad.

I smiled at myself in the mirror and my cheeks shook from the effort. Why was I even fighting this battle with the Tritons? They were consuming me and leaving me a shell of myself.

I sighed and got into the shower. The water calmed me down immensely and I started to feel a little better, but then my mind traveled to *them* again.

Mr. Nguyen had warned me to stay away from them. I ran over the conversation a hundred times a day. He knew small pieces of the puzzle and it was my job to put together.

I wrapped a towel around myself and went back into my room. I laid back on the bed and stared at my ceiling. What was I missing?

The knife.

I rolled over to the other side of the bed and reached under my mattress, sliding it out of the place I had hidden it. I held it in my hand and examined it closely. It was almost as if it was a piece of art with the inlaid designs in the hilt. It made me smile as I turned it over in my hand. Why would my mom have this knife?

A *siren's knife*, Jax had called it when I was hiding in the back of his SUV. What did that mean?

I laid the knife on the bed and opened up my laptop, bringing it with me back to the bed. I pulled up the internet and typed it in. Nothing came up, so I tried *abalone knife*. There were plenty of knifes that had abalone hilts, but none that looked like my mom's.

My mom's looked like it would be used to kill someone. It had a nine-inch blade that curved slightly at the end and it was sharpened to a thin edge that would cut like butter.

Abalone shell was said to have protective properties that would protect from bad intentions. I didn't believe that rocks and minerals had abilities like that though.

I typed in siren, even though I was well aware of the stories of them from Greek mythology. They were dangerous and lured sailors to their deaths. Maybe the knife was an antique object thought to be from them.

I looked at the knife again before sliding it back under the mattress. Mr. Nguyen said not to let anyone know I had it, so my questions would remain a big fat mystery.

THE FIRST SWIM meet of the fall season was jam packed with spectators. I stayed as close as possible to the stands as swimmers dashed past me and readied to swim in their heats.

Even though there were plenty of swim meets for me to take photos, getting the bulk of the shots early was best since the farther I got into the school year, the busier I'd be. Especially with college applications being due anytime between November and January.

During the heats that the Tritons were in, I watched them closely and took plenty of photos and videos. I was fairly certain they were taking some kind of performance-enhancing drug. I was surprised no one had caught on so far.

When they swam, they moved with a fluidity that no one else even came close to matching. From the moment their feet left the blocks to the time they turned at the opposite wall, they barely came up for air.

At first I thought they were breathing, but the more I watched and zoomed in with the camera lens, the more I noticed. With them being in the water and so much action happening, it was hard to tell for sure. They moved their heads, but their mouths didn't open.

Once they won their heats, which was not surprising, they didn't even seem to be out of breath like the rest of the swimmers. It was as if the races had been leisurely walks through the park for them.

The meet lasted hours and I decided to stay the entire time, not taking pictures for yearbook, but to gather evidence against them. I still had the unknown pill hidden in my desk drawer. It was low on my priority list, but there had to be a lab somewhere that would do an analysis of its contents.

Once the meet was over, I hung back in the stands. It was nearly dark, and since most of the ceiling and upper section of the walls were glass, I saw the gorgeous shades of pinks and purples in the sky.

I was in the last little group of people leaving the stands when I heard Jax ask, "Did you find it?"

I continued on with the group, but instead of exiting out into the lobby, I waited until they walked through the doors and then stayed close to the side of the bleachers.

"I looked but it was nowhere to be found," Morgan said.

The bleachers weren't like in the movies. These were state of the art stands that had a wall preventing you from slipping behind. There was a door though. I turned the knob and peeked inside. It was a storage area for lane ropes and other pool equipment.

"Where exactly did you look?" Jax was standing with his arms crossed over his chest.

I could still see the main pool from between the bleachers and the Tritons standing near the edge of it. They were still in their swimming gear.

"Literally every drawer and closet. She has a vibrator, by the way." Morgan laughed when Blake smacked his chest. "What? I thought you'd like to know that the vixen isn't so innocent."

My stomach dropped and I put my hand over my mouth, realizing he had been in my house and must have been looking for the knife. What else would they have been after?

"Are you sure she even had it?" Blake was wringing his hands at his sides and rocking on the balls of his feet.

"Yes, and Mo said that guy mentioned the knife. It has to be real." He ran his hand over his hair and then clamped a hand down on Blake's shoulder to get him to stop moving. "Just wait for the coach to come back through here."

"It hurts." Blake started jumping like he was getting ready for a race.

I couldn't stop myself from looking at their bodies in their swim jammers. It left nothing to the imagination.

"If you had sex more, that would help. Right, Jax?" Morgan laughed and moved away from Blake's fist. "Don't get mad at me for speaking the truth. Our dicks taking a little swim in a mouth or pussy does wonders."

"What are you three still doing here?" The swim coach came out from the locker room area with a bag over his shoulder. "Going to stay and swim some more? If I didn't know any better, I'd say you were born fish."

They all laughed uncomfortably. Jax held up a set of keys and jingled them. "You know it."

"I'll lock the front doors. The locker rooms are clear and the back doors locked. The custodian is cleaning the men's locker rooms."

"Thanks, Coach." Jax threw the keys next to a towel and they waited in silence.

It must have been ten minutes and then all three dived into the water. I moved to the other end of the bleachers to get a better view of the pool.

My heart pounded as none of them resurfaced for air. I saw movement under the water but it was almost dark and they hadn't turned on the lights.

I took my phone out and set it to record. It was so hard to see anything in the dim light. A solid five minutes passed and I turned off my phone and crept back to the door.

What if they were in trouble? Would I be able to jump in and save them?

I exited from under the bleachers and walked toward the pool, which was dark, but I saw shadows moving. My brain didn't quite process the movement. It was much too fast to be human, but it had to be. I had seen them get in the pool.

All of a sudden, a shadow that had been darting through the water burst through the surface and landed on the other side of the pool.

I gasped and stumbled back, luckily correcting my footing before I fell. Had I not been a dancer and quick with my feet and balance, I would have.

It was so dark in the room now that I could only make out his shape. His head snapped around and his eyes met mine.

I'd seen those eyes before.

I screamed and took off toward the nearest door, which was the women's locker room.

I ran through to the outside exit, bumping into a bench on the way. "Fuck," I hissed, grabbing onto my knee. I limped the rest of the distance, the pain from my knee pulsating along with my rapidly beating heart.

I yanked the door open to find Morgan blocking my path, his hands gripping the door frame. Water was dripping down his body and his chest heaved.

How had he made it around the building so fast?

"What are you doing here so late, vixen?" He walked toward me and I backed up.

"I had-" My back hit a wall and he caged me in with his arms. "I forgot something in my locker. My mom is waiting for me in the parking lot."

It was the first thing that came to mind and I

cringed. They didn't know for sure that my mom hadn't returned.

He leaned forward so his mouth was by my ear. "You and I both know your mom isn't waiting for you."

A feeling of dread filled me and I tried to duck under his arm, but he put his arm across my upper chest, pinning me against the wall.

"Let me go." I kicked his shin, but he didn't flinch.

He cocked his head to the side and then leaned in close to my ear again. "What did you see?"

I gasped as his lips brushed against the shell of my ear. "What do you want from me?" I choked on the last word.

He ghosted his lips down my jaw until his face was hovering right in front of mine. He was a mere inch from kissing me.

"What do we want from you?" His voice was deep and breathy, and I bit back a whimper that threatened to escape. "Where's your father?"

"I d-don't know." I stared unblinkingly back at him. "I told you, I've never met him."

He laughed. "I find that hard to believe." He brought his other hand up to my face and cupped my cheek. "Don't make a sound."

Not a second later, one of the doors on the other side of the locker room opened. "Male custodian, any females?"

I opened my mouth to scream, but Morgan had already anticipated it and clamped a hand over my mouth. My screams were muffled and I tried to bite into his hand, but it was impossible.

I pulled at his arms to try to get free, but his upper body was built solid and he didn't move a muscle as the man whistled.

Morgan moved us toward the door and quickly opened it, shoved me outside, and had it shut before a scream could leave me.

I took off at a sprint toward the parking lot, trying to dig my keys out of my bag while running. They wouldn't really physically hurt me, would they?

My car lights blinked twice as I unlocked it and threw the door open, only to have the door slammed before I could get in.

"If it isn't the little minnow, trying to get away from the sharks." Jax made a disapproving sound. "You better run. Morgan likes to play hide-and-seek."

Fear pulsed through my veins and I ran back

toward the gates. My bag slipped off my shoulder, but I ignored it. A bag wasn't worth them catching me.

I heard them laughing, and then the laughing faded away as I came to a stop around the corner of a building in the middle of campus.

I pulled my phone out of my back pocket. "Nine-one-one, what's your emergency?"

"Three guys are chasing me. Please help." I was panicking and peeked around the side of the building. "Please hurry, I'm at Salinity Cove High School."

The operator went through a series of questions and told me to stay calm. She suggested I try to find the custodian, but I was glued to my spot.

I could hear sirens in the distance and a sob escaped as relief flooded my body. They came to a stop in the parking lot.

"Ma'am are you still there? They say to stay where you are and they'll find you."

They found me sitting on the side of the building, shivering uncontrollably. It wasn't even that cold outside, but the adrenaline dump had left me feeling worn out and freezing cold.

An officer sat me in the front of a police car

with a blanket wrapped around me. My bag sat on the pavement in front of my feet, tire marks covering it. I didn't know how I was going to explain to Mr. Garcia that a car had run over it and smashed the expensive camera to smithereens.

"Do you know who was chasing you?" An officer squatted down in front of me and handed me a water bottle.

I took a long drink and shut my eyes. "The Tritons." A deadly calm like I'd never felt before washed over me. "They chased me from the aquatic center."

"The who? The dad from *The Little Mermaid*?" The officer scratched his head.

I wanted to laugh and cry at the same time. Were they mermaids? They couldn't be. Morgan had jumped out of the pool and landed on two feet. But his eyes had been the same as the ones I saw the day I almost drowned.

"Jax West, Blake Huron, and Morgan Wade."

"Those boys? Why would they do this?" He stood and gestured for a man dressed in plain clothes to join us.

"Where is Detective Wilson? I'd been in contact with him about one of them breaking into my house."

"Leave of absence."

"I think I'm going to be sick." I rushed out of the car and made it to the planter just in time.

Chapter Eighteen

*A*fter a weekend of eating too much ice cream and watching the video on my phone from the swimming meet on repeat, a few things had become clear to me: they were on some crazy type of performance enhancers, or they weren't human.

I found myself giggling like a mad woman anytime I thought about them being something other than human. Humans were it. There were no other lifeforms with our level of intelligence.

Or was there?

I didn't want to believe what I had seen in the aquatic center. It could have just been my nerves playing tricks on me. It had been so dark that when Morgan had looked at me, his eyes had flashed to something non-human. Unless it was just a trick of the light or a side effect of taking drugs.

Things were too quiet at school on Monday. I'd come to anticipate something happening and was on edge. I was pretty sure I was developing an ulcer; my stomach was constantly in knots.

Added to that was having to go to yearbook. Every Monday we did a debrief of any photographs taken from the week before and shared the best shots with staff. I had considered sharing the video on my phone, but I didn't have enough evidence to accuse them of anything yet.

As soon as I entered the room, I walked over to Mr. Garcia, who was already powering up his computer and connecting the projector.

"Mr. Garcia. There was an accident over the weekend with the camera." I kept my voice low so no one would hear me. He looked up and waited for me to continue. "I was chased after the swim meet on Saturday night and I dropped the bag. It was run over."

"Chased?" The room behind me fell silent and I felt all eyes on me. "We can always send it to the repair shop."

I pulled the camera bag out of my bag and opened it. "I'm afraid it's damaged beyond repair."

He took the bag from me and looked inside. "This is our best and most expensive camera, Riley."

I guess he had missed the part about me being chased. "I know. I... they were going to hurt me."

He put the camera off to the side and looked up at me. "Did the surveillance get them?"

"The cameras were conveniently rebooting." I turned and looked over my shoulder at Jax. He was sitting with his arms crossed over his chest, glaring at me. I turned back to Mr. Garcia. "I identified them though."

"Did you press charges?"

I twisted my mouth to the side. "No. They said being chased wasn't a crime."

"I can find out how much a replacement would cost and see if we have enough money in our funds to replace it."

"Thank you. I-"

"Mr. Garcia, shouldn't she have to pay for the camera since her negligence broke it? That money is supposed to be to update old equipment." Ashley needed to shut up and go away.

I didn't take my eyes off Mr. Garcia. "I'll take that under consideration. Go sit down. We need to get started."

I kept my eyes down as I went to my computer and sat down. Tory nudged me. "Are you okay?"

"No."

If I had to pay for the camera, I was going to have to start selling furniture.

"WHERE'S MY CAR?" I stared at the empty space where I had parked my car. "This is where I parked it, isn't it?"

Ivy stood next to me and looked around. I had parked right next to her like I normally did. "Do you think they could have..."

I didn't know what to think. So far, the things they'd done to me had been childish. Stealing my car would be stooping to a new low.

"There's only one way to find out." I turned back toward the school with Ivy hot on my heels.

I was angrier than I had ever felt. If I'd had my knife, there was no telling what I'd have done with it. I stopped short and Ivy almost bumped into me.

"What is it?"

I shut my eyes. "I need to calm down."

I took a few deep breaths and then continued to

the aquatic center where the swim team was holding practice.

"What are you going to do?" Ivy was struggling to keep up with me. I told her that wearing wedges wasn't a good choice in footwear. I don't even know how she managed to make it to some of her classes on time. A few were across the campus from each other.

"Confront them." I flung open one of the doors and marched inside. I was still angry, but my stabby feelings had passed, at least for the time being. "Embarrass them."

"Girl, I don't know if it's you that will be embarrassing them." Ivy pulled me to a stop once we were inside the facility. The pool area was only being used by the women's swim team. "They are getting worse. I don't want you to get hurt anymore."

I turned to face her. "My mom is missing and they are tormenting me. What do you want me to do? Just lay down and take it?" I shook my head. "They have souls, Ivy, I've seen it. I just need to make them see that I'm not going to break."

I headed across the facility to the doors leading to the weight room. "You've kind of got the whole angry chick vibe going on right now."

I snorted and pulled open the door. "I have a reason."

"Holy hotness." Ivy's eyes widened as we came to a stop in the doorway.

Most of the guys were shirtless and sweaty. Had I not been pissed off and on a mission, I would have appreciated the view. My eyes were set on finding three assholes that were probably just as shirtless and sweaty.

It was as if I was beckoned by them because I found them clear across the room in the squat racks without skipping a beat. There were some stares as I crossed the room, but most of the swim team was focused on their workouts, or pretending to be.

"Where's my car?" I put my hands on my hips and stood right in the middle of the squat platform.

Morgan had just come out of a squat and walked forward to rack his weight. He wiped his brow with his forearm and I watched him in the mirror.

"Your car?" Blake added a plate on one side of the bar. "What do you mean?"

"My car is missing from the parking lot. Where is it?" I clenched my fists at my sides and reminded myself that I was a calm and collected individual.

"We don't know what you're talking about. Are

you high?" Jax stepped up to the bar and settled it on his back. "You shouldn't be standing there."

I moved to the side as he backed up and started squatting. I didn't know much about squatting, but it looked like it was a lot of weight.

"Maybe I should be asking you that same question. You are the ones taking secret pills."

Jax cursed, and the bar rolled from his back and hit the floor. I backed up a step right into Morgan, who had somehow, in my distracted state, moved right behind me. The heat radiated off his body but sent chills across my skin.

"What are you talking about?" Jax stepped closer and Morgan grabbed my arms, holding me in place.

I looked down at his sweaty chest and gulped. He was too hot for his own good. Maybe I was experiencing something similar to Stockholm syndrome because they were hot.

"The pills in your bag." I lifted my eyes from his chest and looked between him and Blake.

"You've gone crazy." Jax and Blake lifted the bar to re-rack it. "You aren't allowed in here when the team is working out."

"My car. Where is it?"

"We didn't do anything to your car, Riley. We

aren't stupid." Blake laughed. "I take that back. We're a little stupid when it comes to you."

Jax hit him across the chest. "Morgan, get her ass out of here before someone drops a weight on her foot."

I opened my mouth to say something back, but Morgan was already moving me toward the back exit like I was some kind of livestock being herded. Ivy jogged across the room and took my hand, leading me the rest of the way out of the building.

"They're lying," I said through clenched teeth.

I SLID into Ivy's car the next day, and she gave me a smile that didn't reach her eyes. She was worried for me and what the Tritons would do next if I didn't locate my father.

I had to find him, but how? So far everything I had tried was a dead end. He didn't have social media and calls to his company went unanswered.

After stopping for coffee, we drove to school in silence. Coffee was growing on me now that I wasn't getting seven or eight hours of sleep every night. It also made me more alert.

The cameras in the parking lot still weren't

working. I had filed a police report about my missing car, but so far, they had turned up nothing. The Tritons were going to get away with stealing my car.

"I think something is wrong with Aiden." Ivy unbuckled her seatbelt and turned toward me. "He hasn't been himself, even last week. Then yesterday..."

It was unlike Aiden to miss school. He had texted us on Sunday that he didn't feel well and would be absent.

She looked out her front window and then leaned forward a bit. "Holy shit. Look."

Aiden was standing with the Tritons and their groupies. "What the fuck?"

I pulled out my phone and sent him a text. He looked at his phone, but instead of responding, he put it away. My stomach twisted.

"This isn't good." Ivy gripped the steering wheel. "Why would he be hanging out with them?"

"Maybe he just wants to be near Miles." I looked back in their direction and met Jax's stare. "He wouldn't just..."

Would he?

In English, I turned to Aiden, ignoring Blake's

glare from across the room. "What's going on, Aiden?"

Aiden looked at Blake and then down at his notebook. "Later."

The word was barely audible, but I tried to focus on school. This was the exact reason I stayed away from drama; it was distracting. Instead of focusing on what literary devices were being used in a poem, I was thinking about my mom, Aiden, and the three assholes.

The bell rang and snapped me out of my inner turmoil. Mrs. Williams walked over to my desk as everyone else was exiting. I had missed her telling everyone minutes earlier to pack up their belongings.

"What's going on with you?" She looked around the room to make sure the last student was out and sat down in the desk Aiden had vacated. "I see that you're struggling."

"Everything is kind of falling apart right now." I put my notebook in my bag and then looked over at her. "Any adult I tell about it seems to suddenly go on a leave of absence."

"Are they hurting you?" She reached over and put her hand on my forearm. "If they are then you keep telling until someone does something about it."

"They want me to get into contact with my father. They aren't physically hurting me... yet."

"What would three teenage boys want with your father?" She leaned back in the chair as the first student from her next period entered. "I think we should contact their parents."

I frowned and stood, grabbing my bag. "I can't have another adult who cares go on leave. Thank you though."

I left to my next class, wondering if I should contact their fathers somehow. I checked my phone as I went into Psychology, ignoring Blake's stare.

Aiden: I slept with Miles and he filmed it. They are threatening me with it.

I nearly tripped over a chair and half fell into my seat.

Me: That's illegal!

Aiden: I know, but they have threatened to send it to my parents.

I had only met Aiden's parents a few times because he avoided them at all costs, but from what he had told me about them, they were very tradi-tional. If they found out he was gay, especially through a sex tape, they'd kick him out.

Me: What are you going to do?

Aiden: I'm trying to figure it out. Maybe it's good I play into this and see if I can find out things before they do them. I can be undercover.

Me: Be careful.

The last thing I had wanted was for them to drag any of my friends into this.

Chapter Nineteen

RILEY

*I*t turned out my car wasn't stolen, it was repossessed. It was almost laughable what was happening to me.

It had been a week since they'd blackmailed Aiden, and we were waiting for the next thing to happen. I had managed to find contact information for Trident Industries and sent an email detailing what their sons had done to me. There had been no response.

It was our first stay-late for yearbook since we had a deadline approaching for a portion of the fall sports and activities. I was impressed with the work Jax had done so far, considering he was new to the program we used to design the yearbook.

"Food's here." Ashley came to stand in front of

my computer as everyone except Jax got up to go to the adjacent classroom to eat. "I need your money if you're going to eat."

"I brought something to eat." I didn't look up from my computer as she continued to stand on the other side of it. "You can go now."

"Come on, Jax. We're having sushi. I know it's your favorite." She sauntered out of the room and I rolled my eyes.

Jax clicked out of the layout he was on, learning his lesson from when I unplugged his computer and swiveled around to face me. "You've been bringing lunch every day. A peanut butter sandwich and pretzels."

"How do you know or even care?"

He stood and crossed his forearms on the top of my monitor, staring down at me. "Where's your car?"

I didn't answer and made sure to click save on the layout I had open. "It's none of your business."

My chest tightened and I fought the urge to flee. The last thing I needed was for Jax to know that I had absolutely no money. The few thousand that had been in the envelope Mr. Nguyen had given me had gone toward the bills that were necessary like gas, electric, and cell phone. Food was way more expensive than I thought, and I'd rather spend less than a dollar a meal than have sushi or cafeteria food.

"Any word from your mom?"

"No." I gulped back the sudden urge to cry. It had crossed my mind a time or two that they might have done something to her, but after the letter it was clear something bigger was going on.

"So, where are you getting money?" Jax was still leaning on the computer monitor.

I finally looked up at him and worry was etched in his features. Why was he worried? He hated my guts.

"I'm waiting on a judge to approve my extenuating circumstances." I covered my face. "Fuck. Now he's probably going to go on a leave of absence."

"What the hell are you talking about?"

"Detective Wilson and Mrs. Miller both conveniently went on leaves of absence with no return dates once I involved them with this." I moved my hands, not caring that tears were streaming down my cheeks. "I don't know where my father is and he doesn't care about me. Why are you ruining my life?"

"We didn't-"

"Forget it. You know what? I'll just see if I can finish my senior year online or even just get my GED." I logged out of the computer and stood. "Go enjoy your sushi."

"Riley."

I stopped at the door and looked back at him. "Fuck off, Jax."

I was grateful he didn't follow me. I started walking toward my house. It was about five miles and I needed the time to think. The sun was just setting, but I felt fairly safe walking home along the busy streets and highway.

I was about a mile into my walk when a black Maserati pulled over. I groaned in frustration and kept my eyes straight ahead.

Blake rolled down the passenger window as I was passing. "Hey! Get in."

I glared at him and continued on. I didn't want a ride from anyone, especially him. The car rolled up along the shoulder next to me.

"It's almost dark. You shouldn't be walking alone." He stopped ahead of me and got out part-way, leaning on the roof of his car. "Did you hear me?"

I stopped and tightened my grip on the strap of

my bag. "Yes, I heard you. I don't want a ride. Especially from you. Leave me alone."

He cursed and then jogged to catch up with me as I began walking again. "I wasn't giving you the choice." He stood in front of me, blocking my path.

I clenched my teeth and resisted the urge to shove him out of the way. His shoulders were so wide, he practically blocked the entire sidewalk. There was no getting around him.

"I don't want or need a ride. I have two perfectly good feet." I tried walking around him, but he moved to stop me. "Seriously?"

I bit down on my lip to stop myself from having a meltdown. He reached forward and put his hand on the side of my arm. "Come on."

He wasn't going to give up, and I did not want him to haul me over his shoulder like a caveman. I let him guide me to the passenger door. He opened it, and I dropped into the bucket seat with a huff. I'd let him give me a ride, but that didn't mean I had to be pleasant.

He jogged around the front of the car and smiled at me as he got behind the wheel. "See, that wasn't so bad now, was it?"

"Just go." I buckled my seatbelt and crossed my arms.

We were both silent, the music coming from the speakers the only thing keeping it from being too awkward. I saw him out of the corner of my eye stealing glances at me, but I kept my eyes on the road or the side mirror.

The car passed my exit and I sat forward a little. "That was my exit." I was fairly certain he knew where I lived.

"I know. We're going to dinner." He started tapping on the steering wheel to the music. "Jax said you hadn't eaten."

That fucker.

"I don't want to eat dinner with you. You'll probably somehow poison my drink when I get up to wash my hands."

I sat back in my seat again, thinking about what my options were. I had a few hundred dollars left that I could use to call a cab, or I could call Ivy. Aiden wasn't an option since Blake would see him.

"Too bad. We're having dinner and you're going to answer some questions."

"Why the hell would I-"

The chirp of a siren came from behind us and I looked in the side mirror to see a highway patrol car with its lights flashing.

"Fuck." Blake's hands tightened on the steering

wheel and he flipped his blinker on and slowed as he pulled to the shoulder.

"You weren't speeding, were you?"

His jaw was set tight and worry was written across his face as he glanced over at me and put the car in park before turning it off.

"No." He grabbed his phone from the cupholder and pushed a few buttons before putting it back. "Just... don't say anything about me making you come with me. Please."

I didn't respond, and he rolled his window down half of the way, turned on the interior light, and put his hands back on the top of the steering wheel. His eyes were locked on his side mirror as the officer approached.

Blake's breathing was labored as the officer came to a stop outside the window and shined his flashlight down on him. His hand was on his holster.

I'd never been in a car that had been pulled over before, but I didn't think having his hand on his weapon was routine procedure for a traffic stop.

"Do you know why I pulled you over, boy?"

"No, sir." I couldn't see his face, but his voice was serious and trembled slightly. "Sir, I wanted to inform you that once my car was in park and turned off, I turned on my video recorder on my phone."

The officer made a noise of annoyance. "This is a traffic stop, boy, not a shakedown. Unless you're hiding something?"

"I don't mean to offend you by filming. It's in my cupholder and won't interfere with you doing your job."

I sat up a little straighter in my seat. It sounded so rehearsed and my chest burned with the sudden realization that this was reality for Blake. I would have never even thought to record an interaction with the police.

"One of your taillights is out." The officer looked over at me. "Where are you two headed this evening?"

Blake's jaw ticked. "Just headed to grab a bite to eat. Just got done at Salinity Cove High with our extracurriculars."

"Young lady?" His eyes were locked on me and I met his questioning eyes. "Where are you headed to eat?"

"We haven't decided yet."

He studied me for what felt like entirely too long before his attention was back on Blake. "Let me see your license and registration."

"Sir, I'm going to reach for my wallet in my cupholder to get my license and grab my registration and insurance from my visor."

Blake passed the documents through the window and the office looked at them. "Mr. Huron. You seem nervous. Is there anything in the car I need to know about?"

"No, officer."

"So, you won't mind if I take a look?" Tears sprang to my eyes and I sat on my hands, resisting the urge to give the man a piece of my mind.

"I don't consent to searches." Blake was calmer than I would have been. "Sir, am I free to go, or are you going to give me a ticket for my taillight?"

With a grunt, the officer walked back to his vehicle. Blake cursed under his breath and kept his eyes on the rearview mirror.

"Blake, what's going on?" I reached over to touch his arm and he pulled away, all the while keeping his hands on the steering wheel.

"Just... be quiet," he whispered.

The officer returned a few minutes later. "I'm going to let you go with a warning this time. Get that taillight fixed." He looked over at me again. "Have a nice evening."

Blake put his papers back in his visor with

shaky hands and turned off the cell phone before starting the car and pulling back onto the highway.

We rode in silence and took the next exit. He pulled into the far end of a parking lot and parked.

"Get out and go behind my car to check my taillights." He stared straight ahead without looking at me.

"What? Why?"

"Just do it, Ri."

I unhooked my seatbelt and got out of the car, hoping he wasn't going to do something crazy like leave me behind.

"Do they work?" He pressed the brakes a few times and flicked both blinkers.

"Everything works."

As if he didn't believe me, he got out and came to stand next to me. "Get in the car and press the brakes and the blinker."

"Is that really-"

"Yes! It's fucking necessary!"

I did as he asked and got back out. He just stood there, staring at the back of his car. I shifted from one foot to another and he finally looked at me, his eyes holding a pain I didn't understand.

I took a step toward him and he backed up,

turning and heading away from me. "Blake! Where are you going?"

"I need a minute." I barely heard him, but stopped myself from following him.

He got to a stray plastic cart, pushed it on its side and gave it a few kicks. He righted it and laced his hands behind his head, his back heaving.

I leaned against the trunk of his car and wondered if there was anything I could say to him to ease his pain and frustration. A million questions flitted through my mind about what had just happened.

A few minutes passed before he turned back around and headed toward the car. He didn't make eye contact or say a word as he got in. I scrambled to the passenger side and got in as he revved his engine.

"I'll take you home."

"What about dinner?"

"I'm not hungry."

He turned the music up loud enough where I couldn't talk and peeled out of the parking lot.

About fifteen minutes later, we pulled into my driveway and he turned off the car, turning toward me. "Do you understand what happened back there?"

"He pulled you over because you're black."

He looked out the front window at the garage door. "My father warned me that the people... the police... wouldn't care how rich I am or what my last name is."

I put my hand on his arm and this time he let me. "You could report him."

He snorted. "And what are you going to do? Testify that my brake lights were fine?"

"If I need to."

"It won't matter. In that officer's eyes, I'm just a black man in an expensive car, driving through a rich town with a white girl in my passenger seat. I can't wait for this year to be over to go back to where I'm not judged." He pinched the bridge of his nose.

"Where is that?"

"Nowhere. Forget I said anything." He looked down at my hand on his arm. "You should get inside."

"Do you want to come in and work on homework or something?" I just wanted to make sure he was okay.

His eyes met mine. "Or something?" The corner of his mouth pulled up. Typical guy. "I thought you hated me."

"It's complicated." It was more complicated than I'd care to admit to him. "Thought you could use the distraction from... life."

I could use the distraction as well. For whatever reason, sitting in the car with him, despite what had just happened, had made me feel calm. I was probably just going crazy.

"I can come in for a bit."

He followed me to the door, and once we were inside, we dropped our bags. "I'd offer a tour, but you already know your way around, don't you?"

"I don't know what you're talking about." He flopped down on the couch and patted the seat next to him. "Let's talk."

My stomach growled and I pulled my uneaten dinner out of my bag. "Want a sandwich?" I unwrapped it and bit into it.

He grabbed it from me as I sat down and took a bite of it, scrunching his face. "It's drier than a piece of beached seaweed."

"That's an interesting comparison." I laughed and took the sandwich back, handing him the small bag of pretzels. "It fills me up."

"Do you not have any money?" He popped a pretzel in his mouth. "Jax said-"

"Why is he pretending he cares?" I put the half-eaten sandwich on the coffee table. "One minute you guys are threatening my best friend with a sex tape, and the next you're showing concern for me. It's like you have multiple personalities."

"We could say the same about you." He took a few more pretzels and threw the bag on the table. "One minute you hate our guts, the next you're inviting us into your house."

I pulled my leg up on the couch and turned toward him. "I'm going to ask you a question and I want you to answer me honestly."

He pulled his own leg onto the couch, his shin touching mine. "Depends what you're about to ask me."

"I saw you, Morgan, and Jax swimming that night." He was going to think I was crazy. "And I filmed it."

"Of course you did." He stood, looking down at me. "It wasn't on that camera?"

Before I could stop him, he reached for my bag and started looking for my cell phone. "It's not in there, and even if it was, I'm not stupid."

"You just told me you had a recording of us. That's pretty stupid." He dropped my bag and laced his hands behind his head again like he'd done in the parking lot. "You need to destroy it."

"Why?" I planted both feet on the ground and looked up at him. He didn't even know what I'd gotten on video.

"If anyone sees..." He started pacing in front of the entertainment center. "All it takes is the wrong person seeing us and that's it."

"What would happen?"

He stopped his pacing and sat back down before taking my face in his hands. The second his hands were on me, something low in my gut stirred. "You didn't see?"

"See what? You were swimming unnaturally fast and Morgan's eyes..."

"What about his eyes?"

"They were glowing yellow and looked weird. If you guys are on drugs that do that to you..."

He sat back, breaking contact with my skin. I frowned down at his hands, wanting them back on me.

He wasn't giving me the answers I wanted. "What do you know about sirens?"

"What do *you* know about sirens? You have a siren knife."

We stared at each other. I was gauging how much I could trust him about the knife and he seemed to be doing the same. Finally, he took my hand and my shoulders relaxed a little.

"All of those knives should have been destroyed a long time ago. They're dangerous in certain hands." I nodded, urging him to continue. "Forget whatever shit you've read from Greek mythology. That's not what sirens really are."

"What are they then?"

"They *were* warriors of the sea. Their purpose was on the front lines, protecting Poseidon's sea palaces from being discovered and infiltrated by explorers. One word from their lips could entrance anyone into forgetting their own name if they wished it." He stood again and went to look out the front blinds. "Poseidon gifted them with knives that had hilts of abalone to sooth their more vicious nature. The knives themselves could cut through anything, including the same doors they were meant to protect."

I wanted to laugh at what he was telling me, because it sounded outlandish. "You said they were warriors?"

"The tritons destroyed their knives and killed them because they attempted to infiltrate the palace to take Poseidon's child."

"Percy Jackson?" I couldn't stop myself from smiling. I was enjoying this story he was telling.

Blake rolled his eyes. "I'm not making this up. Poseidon thought he was immune to the sirens, but he was wrong."

"Are sirens blue?" I still didn't understand how it all connected, or what my estranged father and my missing mom had to do with it all.

He turned back to the window again and didn't answer. I stood and went to stand beside him. Jax's SUV was sitting out front.

"They aren't blue." His frown deepened as Jax got out of his vehicle and leaned against the passenger side, staring right at us. "Tritons are blue... for camouflage."

Jax pushed off the side of his car and walked toward the front door, a scowl on his face. I didn't know what he thought he was doing, but I wasn't about to let him in my house so they could outnumber me.

"Are you going to let him in?" Blake's laugh was uncomfortable. "He'd love to hear you ask all these questions about sirens and tritons."

The doorbell rang. "Will he tell me what the hell is really going on?"

"Only one way to find out." Blake sat back

down on the couch. "If you don't let him in, he'll find a way in."

I scoffed and went to the door, taking a deep breath before opening it. "What do you want?"

He walked in and pushed past me. "Blake. Why are you here?"

"Just hanging out. What are *you* doing here?"

They stared at each other and then both looked at me. I wasn't sure why I'd let either of them into my house.

"Blake was telling me about sirens and tritons." I crossed my arms.

"Was he now?" Jax moved toward me and I backed into the wall. "And what conclusions did you come to?"

I gulped as his hands went on either side of me on the wall, caging me in. "Are you three..."

"What, Riley? Are we what?" His head was cocked to the side in question and his blue eyes darkened. "Say it."

I gulped and tried to look past him to Blake, but he grabbed my chin. My skin heated with his touch, and I leaned harder against the wall, using it for support.

It was taking everything in me not to kiss him and I didn't know why. "Are you... sirens?"

Jax's lips turned up as he let go of my chin and ran a finger over my lips. "Sirens are female, and so incredibly intoxicating, males lose their minds with one little taste of her lips. Sometimes even the sound of her voice." He cocked his head to the side. "Where's the knife?"

"What?" I had been so mesmerized by his fingers tracing my lips that I couldn't think. "The knife?"

"Go get the knife." He pushed away from me and sat down next to Blake. "We'll be waiting."

Chapter Twenty

JAX

*A*s soon as she was far enough up the stairs, I turned to look at Blake. His lips were drawn in a tight line and his shoulders slumped.

"Are you worried she has siren in her bloodline? It's highly unlikely." Even as I said the words, they sounded ridiculous.

What I felt toward Riley wasn't normal. She was like a magnet and I couldn't get her out of my head. Tritons, both male and female, didn't feel the kind of desire that I had for her. I wanted to take her to my bed, tie her up, and never let her go. Or let her tie me up.

"I'm not worried about that." He sat back on the couch and rubbed the stubble on his cheek. "A highway patrol pulled me over for no reason. Was a real dick."

"Did you get his badge number? They should know-"

"It was because of my skin color, Jax." I rolled my eyes. It was still a fairly new phenomenon for me since I had only been on land just over three years. "If they treat black people and other people of color like criminals, how would they treat non-humans?"

"Not well. We can't let Riley know." Of that I was sure. We needed to be more careful around her.

"She knows we're something, but seems to be in denial." He stood. "What's taking her so long?"

I cursed and followed him up the stairs. I went straight to her room where the door was shut and opened it.

"What the hell?" Blake took a step in and then thought better of it and stepped back out.

In our human form, we weren't as strong or as well protected as when we were shifted. In the water, we were not only able to camouflage to be virtually undetectable to human eyes, but we had a layer of protective scales.

The scales protected us against most threats, including shark bites, but there was one thing that it

didn't protect us from: a siren's knife. The same
knife that Riley was standing in the middle of the
room with. Her eyes landed on us as her chest
heaved.

I wasn't sure what Blake had told her before I
arrived, but clearly she had decided to test out its
capabilities on her desk chair, wall, and a wooden
storage box at the end of her bed. It looked like she
had stabbed it about twenty times.

"Can you put the knife down?" I held up my
hands and stepped toward her. I hoped she didn't
plan on coming at me with it. "I guess we now know
you have a little siren blood in you."

She held the knife out at me like the night I had
let myself into her house and room. "Stay back."

Blake's cell phone rang with Morgan's ringtone.
He ignored it and stepped beside me. "Riley, this
changes things."

Her eyebrows pinched together and she backed
up. "No, it doesn't. You took my mom, didn't
you?"

"We didn't." I kept my eyes locked on hers. I
could see how she would draw that conclusion, but
we weren't monsters.

"Then who did?" Her chin trembled, but she
quickly pulled herself together and stood up

straighter. "You three are mermaids and I can stab crap I shouldn't be able to stab with this knife."

She stepped to her bed and slashed at the metal spindle on the end. It flew off and hit the wall on the other side of the room. A pained laugh left her.

"Why don't you put the knife down and we can talk about this." Blake stepped toward her again, but this time the bed was between us and her.

"So you can take the knife and destroy it?" She was back to pointing it at us. "Fuck that."

I rubbed the back of my neck. "You know too much."

"So what, are you going to kill me now like some mafia boss?" She pulled her phone out of her back pocket. "I'm calling the police."

"The police won't help you. The chief is one of us, and if he sees that knife, I can guarantee he'll tell the admiral." I crossed my arms over my chest. "If the admiral knows you know about us, he *does* act like a mafia boss."

"So you're military?" I was glad I confused her. She needed to be confused about what we were.

"Something like that." I jumped a bit when Morgan's ringtone sounded in my pocket.

"You should get that, it might be the *admiral*."

I picked up the second time it went off. "What?"

"It's your sister."

There were few things that shook me to my core. One was thinking about my mother, and another was the possibility of my sister joining my mother.

I took off down the stairs, Blake right behind me. I knew I was in no state to drive so I headed to his car, which was faster anyway.

"Where are you going?" Riley was in the door-way, knife in hand, looking confused.

I rounded the car and opened the passenger door before speaking. "You better pray, Kline, because if my sister-"

"Jax. Get in." Blake was the definition of calm as he gave me a warning look over the top of the car. "It's not her fault."

I got in and slammed the car door as Blake started the engine. I shut my eyes and hoped my sister hadn't taken a turn for the worse.

Chapter Twenty-One

RILEY

*T*he Tritons weren't at school on Thursday and Friday. I had texted all three and got no response. I didn't know why I cared, but it felt important to keep tabs on them at all times.

I had tested the knife on countless things, including the marble counter in the kitchen. It cut through it like it wasn't a solid piece of rock. The imaginative side of me wondered if it could cut through a bank vault.

My phone rang right as school got out on Friday. It was Mr. Nguyen, who I hadn't heard from him since we met about the secret money my mom had stashed away.

After exchanging brief pleasantries, he got

straight to the point. "The judge who was supposed to sign off on releasing the money to you went out on a leave."

I stopped and leaned against the bank of lockers, shutting my eyes. "I needed that money. They already took my car."

"These boys you're dealing with, their families do not like your father." I heard a door close on his end of the phone. "How much has your mother told you?"

"Nothing. How do you know anything about what's happening?" I was starting to grow suspicious of every single person now.

If the Tritons could pay off security at the school, just what else were they capable of? I knew that had to have something to do with where my mom was and the financial issues I was now going through.

"I was good friends with your mom in high school." He sounded distraught. "But as soon as she left Finn and started seeing Robert, she changed."

"Changed how?" My feet carried me toward the parking lot where Ivy was waiting.

"Cut off ties with everyone, and Robert became her sole focus. I hadn't heard from her in years until she came to my office one day with you when you were just a few months old."

I slid into Ivy's car and turned down the music. She gave me a questioning look and then pulled out of the parking lot and drove toward the dance studio where she would drop me off.

"Did she share anything else with you besides what you told me already?" I looked at the dark clouds in the distance and thought it was fitting to my mood lately.

"She said that Robert had dangerous information about Finn, you, and her. She was scared he was going to do something if she stepped out of line and she wanted to set up a safeguard for you just in case."

"What information about Finn?"

"She told me it had something to do with his family and her family. She gave me as little information as possible because she feared he would find out and come after me. Those with money will do anything to protect their names and themselves." He cursed. "I have to go. I'm working on getting this in front of another judge."

He hung up and I stared at my phone. "Fuck." I shut my eyes and then slammed my fist against the dashboard, causing Ivy to swerve a bit.

"Hey, what's wrong?" She reached over and put her hand on my arm.

"What isn't wrong, Ivy?" I choked on my tears as they started falling. I wanted to be strong because that's what my mom would have wanted, but I was scared. "When are they going to get to you and take you away from me?"

The sheer loneliness I felt from not having my mom around was suffocating me. I never realized how much I relied on her for emotional support until she wasn't there to listen to me or for me to hear her stories.

"I promise you they won't. I don't care if they film me taking a shit. Let them post it on the internet." She turned into the dance studio parking lot.

I laughed and started coughing. She rubbed my back and handed me her water bottle. "Thanks."

"Aiden will come back to us. If only he was still seventeen he could go to the police for child pornography." She turned toward me. "Speaking of seventeen. Your birthday is next Saturday. Do you still want to have a kickback party?"

I put my head back against the headrest and wiped at my face with a tissue. "I don't know. My electricity might not even be working by then."

"I can talk to my parents about letting you

borrow some money." Ivy had already done so much for me and my tab was over five hundred dollars with her.

It wasn't that I was opposed to accepting her help, but the way things were looking, it didn't seem I'd ever get access to the money in the account my mom had set up. She had it set to pay out to me when I graduated college or with a judge's approval in a time of need. That was probably the only way she could protect it from my father.

"I might not be able to pay them back for a while." Another round of tears hit me. "How am I going to pay for college applications?"

"Let me talk to them, okay?" She leaned across the console and pulled me into a hug.

I didn't know how I had gotten so lucky to have a friend like her. I just hoped I didn't lose her by the time everything was over.

The sound of a motorcycle coming to park next to us made me pull away. Morgan sat on his bike, looking over at the car with his helmet still in place. I could practically feel his eyes boring into me through his tinted visor.

"I thought you told Bernardo you didn't want him as a partner." Ivy sat back in her seat with a huff. "It's like they want to make you miserable but can't do it from afar."

I considered confiding in her about the knife and the strong possibility that I was some kind of distant relative of sirens. It would be so much easier if she knew.

There was a reason the Tritons acted fearful of the knife. I would never be able to use it on a person, but its possibilities were constantly on my mind. Not that I'd ever go on a jewel heist or rob a bank.

I flung open my door and stepped out. I gave a quick wave to Ivy as she pulled away. She had volleyball practice, but Bernardo already said he'd give me a ride home since he didn't have a lesson after mine.

I ignored Morgan and walked into the studio. The tightness in my chest instantly decreased as the familiar smell of suede hit my nose.

Bernardo came from around the front desk and pulled me into a hug as soon as he looked up from the computer screen. "Go get changed and let's dance it all away."

He knew it was my last lesson for a while. The owners were still going to let me come to dance classes and practice parties, but it wouldn't be the same as learning in a one-on-one format.

I said hello to another student and instructor on my way to the bathroom. I set my bag on the bench in the bathroom and pulled my shirt over my head. Just as it was completely off, the door opened and I turned my back.

"Sorry, I've gotten too comfortable around here." I laughed and pulled a thinner, more practice-worthy shirt over my head.

"Do you always just change out in the open like this?"

My body froze and my face turned fifty shades of pink. I was lucky I hadn't had my pants off. "It has a picture of Ginger Rogers and the word *women* right on the door. Most men don't just walk into a women's restroom."

I turned to face him and had to stop myself from having a reaction to the way he looked. He was leaning with his shoulder against the door, his legs crossed. His hair fell onto his forehead and he brushed it back with his free hand.

That wasn't the most drool worthy part about him. He was dressed head to toe in leather that hugged him in all the right places. I resisted the urge to look south of his waist.

"Do you like what you see?" He pushed off the door and put his helmet down on the bench before shrugging out of his leather jacket. Underneath, he wore a skin-tight black shirt and my mouth opened a bit.

My body didn't seem to get the message that he was the enemy.

"Bernardo said he had some clothes for me to change into since apparently leather isn't that easy to move in. I tried to explain to him that in the bedroom I move just fine in leather."

My eyes went wide and I grabbed my skirt. "He probably took that as a come on."

He moved to block my path into the one and only stall. "Going somewhere, vixen?"

"To change." My eyes deceived me and slipped down past his waist. The leather sat snug against his muscular quadriceps, and it was clear he was happy about something. "If you're looking for *men's* clothing to change into, it's across the hall. Unless you want to wear my skirt."

He hooked his fingers in my belt loops and pulled me against him. "I haven't seen you in a few days. I missed you."

"What are you even doing here?" I backed away from him and stepped into my skirt, taking my jeans off under it. "Shouldn't you be brushing your mermaid hair with a fork?"

I turned to put my pants in my bag, but he pushed me against the wall, his mouth coming to my ear. "Do I need to tell you not to say shit like that out loud?"

"Let me go."

"Not until you tell me you understand." His lips were right against the shell of my ear, and I shuddered. "Does this excite you? Me pressed up against you like this?"

I couldn't find my voice as he moved his hips closer and I felt his excitement against my ass. He let out a confused laugh when I didn't respond. "I guess I'll go find those clothes to change into."

I had to sit down on the bench for a few minutes before going back into the studio. I hadn't wanted to believe that I was a siren, but damn it if I didn't feel like doing stupid shit when they were near.

It didn't explain why it was only around them, but I also had a knife that could cut through metal and marble without much effort on my part. Maybe I was dreaming and would wake up.

I splashed water on my face and looked in the mirror. My face was splotchy from crying and there were circles under my eyes. I needed a weekend where I didn't have to worry about where my mom was or what I was going to do when the money ran out.

I needed to get a job.

The reality of it set in again, and I closed my eyes. I could handle this. I was practically eighteen and was going to be away at college next year anyway. Growing up was just coming a little sooner than expected.

There was a knock on the door. "We're waiting!" Bernardo couldn't hide the excitement in his voice.

I took a deep breath and walked into the studio.

I HADN'T WANTED to be rude when my last lesson was spent practicing the waltz with Morgan, so I let my annoyance fester inside. He had distracted my focus to the point where I could hardly move without messing up a step.

He had changed into sweatpants that were way too tight on him, but were better than the leather he had been sporting. I even caught Bernardo checking out his ass a few times in the mirror as we moved across the floor.

Morgan *was* a natural at dance, but I couldn't figure out how he learned the steps and how to move correctly so quickly. It usually took me an entire lesson to get a new step learned and integrated to be fluid, and he could do it after seeing Bernardo model it once.

The end of the lesson came too soon, and Bernardo took my arm and led me and Morgan to the office and shut the door. He slid a box of tissue over to me as we sat since tears were already silently falling down my cheeks.

I was going to set a world record for crying in one day at the rate I was going.

Morgan sat hunched over with his forearms on his knees and watched me as I tried to pull myself together.

"I know today was officially supposed to be our last lesson, but Morgan came by earlier and talked with me." Bernardo gave Morgan a look of endearment. "He has offered to pay for lessons for the both of you as partners."

I looked at Morgan, who was smiling at me. "Why?"

He rolled his eyes and sat back in his chair, propping his ankle onto his knee. "Can't I just do something nice for you?"

"No." I stood. "This last lesson was supposed to be special and you completely took it over!"

Bernardo looked taken aback and looked between Morgan and me. "Riley, he's just trying to help."

"I don't need his help. He probably just wants sex." I crossed my arms and glared down at Morgan. "Or to ruin the only good thing I had left."

He threw his hands up in surrender before lacing them together on his stomach. "So you'd rather not dance than accept my offer?"

I worked my bottom lip between my teeth. Would it really be so bad to take dance lessons with him?

"What's in it for you?" I sat back down, the fight leaving my body. I was tired of fighting. "I won't be able to pay you back, at least not anytime soon."

"Nothing." His eyes twinkled, really bringing out the green flecks in his hazel eyes. "I just want to dance."

"What about swimming?" *What about you being a fucking mermaid or whatever the hell you are?*

"I can do both. You do this and yearbook." He looked at Bernardo. "Two lessons a week and put us down for Hawaii."

"What?" I blinked at him. "I can't-"

Morgan slid a credit card across the desk. "I can and I will. We're doing this, vixen."

I sat back in my chair and met Bernardo's questioning stare. "Fine."

When the time came, I just wouldn't go.

Chapter Twenty-Two

MORGAN

*J*ax was going to kill me when I told him I was now Riley's official dance partner and we'd be spending a lot of hours with our bodies pressed close. He'd already told us multiple times that she was his, but she hadn't claimed him yet, so it was fair game.

After changing back into my leather, I waited near the door for Riley to change. Bernardo was supposed to give her a ride home, but I had other plans.

"Ready to roll?" I asked when she was almost to me. Her face scrunched up and I laughed. "I'll let you wear my helmet."

"I'm not getting on that death rocket with you."

She leaned her arms on the counter, giving me her back.

I took that as an opportunity to move right beside her and wrap an arm around her waist. "It'll be fun. Bernardo lives in the opposite direction." I smirked as she spun toward me. Now she was even closer.

I knew that part of what might be causing my attraction to her was the fact that she was some percentage of siren. Blake and Jax didn't know much about sirens themselves, so we were left with a lot of questions about her.

It's not like we could go and start asking questions about sirens. She'd be killed.

"He does have a point." Bernardo wiggled his eyebrows. "I have some paperwork to do anyway. It would be better if he took you."

"Thanks a lot." She shoved off the counter and headed out the door, pulling her phone from her bag. "I'll just call someone else to come get me."

"Who? Ivy has practice, the rest of your friends are too scared, and Aiden doesn't want his ass plastered everywhere."

"I'll walk then." She tried to walk past me and I caught her around the waist, pulling her to me. Her hands landed on my chest, but she didn't push away. "I don't want to ride with you."

"What are you so scared of?" She bit her lip and I used my thumb to free it from her teeth. "I'll even go the speed limit."

She stared at my bike for a moment and then at me. "You'll go under the speed limit and get in the slow lane."

"I knew you'd cave." I grabbed her hand and pulled her over to my Ninja. "All you have to do is hold on. I'll do all the work."

I helped her put the helmet on and climbed on the bike. I patted the small space behind me and scooted forward so she could get situated. "Just wrap your arms around my waist and hold on tight."

The second her arms went around me, I scooted back and started my bike. I felt the heat between her legs against my ass and pressed a palm against my growing erection before pulling out of the parking space and turning onto the street.

She held onto me tight enough that if I didn't have my leather jacket on, she'd have drawn blood. She was tense for the first few minutes, but then slowly relaxed and her grip loosened a bit.

I sped up and I could practically feel her heartbeat against me as I pulled onto the highway. Her house wasn't far from the dance studio, but instead of pulling off at her exit, I continued on. She squeezed me but didn't have any choice but to go with me.

The sun was setting and through the trees and houses off the highway, the ocean glittered in the fast retreating light of the day. We'd had to miss swim practice in the morning and my muscles were aching to feel the water.

The highway curved inland and I took the first turn down the road to our house, back toward the ocean. The road was shrouded in trees, and unless you really were looking for it, you couldn't see the dirt path.

The gate opened for me automatically and the road turned to pavement as I pulled into the garage and turned off the bike.

She ripped the helmet off her head, her hair sticking to her forehead with a light sheen of sweat. "What the fuck are we doing here?"

I took my helmet from her before she used it as a weapon against me. "It's Friday night, vixen. You don't want to spend it alone, do you?"

"I certainly don't want to spend it with you."

She stomped over to the door leading into the house. "I'll call an Uber to come get me."

"Ubers won't come here." I reached around her, putting in the four-number code to unlock the door. It didn't escape my notice that she watched me do it. I'd have to change it later. "Come on. I'll cook you a nice dinner. We can go swimming, maybe Netflix and chill."

"Netflix and chill," she deadpanned. For being so against me bringing her to the house, she followed me inside without complaint. "So you can videotape it and use it as a threat?"

I stopped just before we got to the living room and she bumped into me. "I would never do that."

"Oh, but hanging my panties and bra up for the entire school and world to see is okay?" She shoved at my back and I turned to face her. "You have some nerve acting like a knight in shining armor today."

"Do you want the alternative?" I spread my arms across the hallway, putting my hands on each wall as she tried to move past me. "Because I can promise you, it won't be pleasant."

"It's already unpleasant." She moved her hair off her forehead. "It's not like you'd hurt me."

I moved to trap her against the wall as she tried

to duck under my arm. "We won't, but that doesn't mean the others wouldn't. They'd torture you until you were an inch from death."

"You don't scare me." She was feistier than usual. I liked it.

"I should."

She looked down at my chest and then cleared her throat. "What are you cooking for dinner?"

I knew my words about torture bothered her, but they were true. If Jax's father found out we had all been having second thoughts about what the fuck we were doing, he'd step in. I didn't even want to imagine his reaction to her being able to use a siren's knife.

Jax's dad was the last person we needed to get involved.

Chapter Twenty-Three

I sat at the kitchen island as Morgan moved around the kitchen. He was making shrimp alfredo, which he said was his specialty.

He bent over to get a pan from a cabinet near the stove and I couldn't help my look as the leather pants stretched tight over his ass and hamstrings. I shouldn't have been checking him out, but when he bent over, it was right there in my face practically begging me to.

"Do you like garlic?" He put the pan on the stove and adjusted the heat on the boiling linguine noodles. "I like a lot, but if you don't like it, I can put less."

"Put less." I loved garlic, but the last thing I

wanted was for my breath to smell. Not that it mattered what my breath smelled like. My eyes went to his lips and I inwardly chastised myself.

He smirked and I slid off the barstool, needing some air. I walked across the living room to the sliding doors he had opened the second we were in the room. The coolness of the air hit my skin and I grabbed the throw blanket off the couch and wrapped it around myself before stepping outside.

The outside of their house was even more impressive than the inside. It seemed like they lived right in the middle of the ocean. I kept a safe distance from the giant pool that had lounge chairs and other outdoor furniture around it, and stopped a few feet away from the railing at the edge of the cliff.

I wasn't scared of heights, but the water on the other side of the glass barrier scared the crap out of me. I took a calming breath and inched forward until I was right at the railing.

The sky was darker than usual with an approaching rainstorm, and the waves crashing against the cliff face below sent a light mist into the air. It was breathtaking, but also terrifying. Someone could easily be thrown over and plummet to their death.

I turned back toward the house. Almost the entire back was floor to ceiling windows. My eyes traveled to Jax's bedroom, and even though the window for the bathroom was tinted so you couldn't see in, I could imagine him standing there on a daily basis, his hand stroking his cock.

Jesus. Get it together, girl.

Shaking my head, I walked back to the house where Morgan was tossing sauce, shrimp, and noodles in a sauté pan. His muscles flexed along his arm and shoulder as he flicked his wrist.

"Why don't you get a few bowls out for us." He raised his chin to a cabinet to his left without looking back at me.

"Have you ever thrown anyone over the railing?" I opened a few cabinets before finding pasta bowls.

Their cabinets were clean and organized with white dishes. I had expected a hodgepodge of various plates and bowls. For being teenage boys, they were tidy.

"Are you offering to be the first?" When my jaw dropped open, he threw his head back and laughed. "We dive off it during high tide."

"But how do you not... die?" I took the bowl he

had served for me and grabbed a few forks from the silverware drawer.

"I think you know why." We sat down at the seats at the island. "If you don't like it, we have a frozen pizza I can throw in the oven."

I spun my fork in the noodles and stabbed a shrimp. As soon as the food hit my tongue, I moaned. It was more delicious than any upscale seafood restaurant could make.

"It's so good!" I took another bite, not even bothering to waste time making a presentable bite.

Morgan flashed me an award-winning smile that almost made me choke. "I went out and caught the shrimp this morning."

"In your boat?" I already knew the answer, but part of my brain still refused to believe they were... aquatic creatures.

"Nope. Not in a boat." The smile didn't leave his face as he dug into his own bowl of pasta. It was hard to imagine them as anything other than human. I should have felt more panicked or shocked, but I also read way too much paranormal romance.

After eating and putting the dishes in the dishwasher, I stood awkwardly by the island. The rain was falling now and the lights had turned on in the living room, casting a romantic glow across the space. Through the windows, I saw the pool lit up with blue lighting, and steam was coming off the top.

"Ready to swim?" He walked around the island and put his hands on either side of me, pinning me against it. "The pool is heated."

I looked past him at the pool. "I don't do water, and I don't have a swimsuit."

His head tilted to the side. "You're scared of the water." It wasn't a question. "Why?"

A small bead of sweat worked its way down my back at his nearness, and the fact we were talking about swimming made my skin heat. "I almost drowned when I was seven."

He made a disbelieving noise and moved back, reaching behind his neck and pulling his shirt off. My lips parted and I sucked in a breath of air. I had seen them all without their shirts, even up close. There was something about being close enough to touch him and there being no one else around that made me feel the need to clench my legs together.

"You have siren in you. Even if it was one percent, there's no way you'd drown. You're aquatic." He moved his hand down his chiseled chest and abs to the button on his pants.

He knew exactly what he was doing and I kept my eyes on his hand as he undid the button and pulled down the zipper.

"A blue creature saved me."

He stopped pulling his pants down. "What?"

I looked up, meeting his heated gaze. "I was pulled out to sea by a rip current and a blue creature with cat eyes put me on a buoy. I think that's what happened since, when I woke, he was staring at me."

"That's impossible." He pulled his pants off, leaving him in a pair of tight boxer briefs that had anchors on them.

"Maybe I was hallucinating."

"Maybe." He moved back toward me. "I'll leave my boxers on for you. What are we going to do about all these clothes?" He ran a hand over my bare arm and my skin broke out in goosebumps.

"I'm not swimming." I crossed my arms, breaking our connection. "I'll just..."

"I promise you won't drown." He took my hand and pulled me toward the doors. "Look how inviting that water looks."

"How deep is it?" I couldn't believe I was considering getting in the pool. There weren't even any steps or a ladder. It was just a rectangle.

"Ten feet." My eyes widened. "There's a ledge inside you can sit on. I swear on baby sharks that I will not let anything happen to you."

Despite everything, I felt the sincerity in his voice. "Fine."

He reached for the hem of my tank and I batted his hand away. "I'm not taking off my clothes."

"Clothes are the worst thing you can have on if you expect not to drown. How is your bra and panties any different than a bikini?"

I was not the bikini wearing type. If I did swim and have a swimsuit, it would be a one piece with shorts. It wasn't that I hated my body, but I also didn't want it hanging out all over the place.

"Fine." I backed up a few steps and pulled my tank and shorts off, leaving them on the floor.

"Damn, vixen." His eyes traveled up and down my body a few times. "I just want to bend you over the back of the couch right now and-"

"Don't." I walked past him into the rain that was still falling, but not as hard as a few minutes prior. "Where is this ledge?"

I sat on the edge of the pool, not ready to get in yet. It was a big step for me to get into a large amount of water again by my own free will.

Morgan dove off the side and made a few laps

before swimming up to me and parting my legs. I went to pull back, but his hands wrapped around my calves and pulled me closer.

"Get in." His eyes smoldered and I scooted closer, sliding into the pool as he grabbed me around the waist.

My butt hit the seat. Morgan leaned in and brushed his lips over mine quicker than I could react and then darted under the water.

He swam the entire length of the pool and then surfaced like he was some kind of Greek god. "How long can you hold your breath?"

"A while." He pushed back off the side and swam two lengths of the pool before joining me on the seat.

"You're a mermaid." I'd said it a few times now, but none of them had corrected me.

He scoffed. "Mermaids like you're thinking of don't exist."

"Mo! What the fuck are you doing?" Jax's voice boomed from inside the house and he stalked toward us. "What the hell is she doing here?"

I'd almost forgotten he hated me and my shoulders fell a little. Morgan noticed and frowned at me before glaring at Jax.

"We're enjoying each other's company. Maybe

you should join us and pull the piece of coral out of your ass."

Jax glared at both of us before storming off. He was the moodiest man I'd ever seen. One minute he seemed like he might be warming up to me, and the next he was looking at me like I had tentacles. I didn't even know why I cared, but the feeling in my stomach told me I cared too much.

"Why does he hate me?" I ran my hands over the water, trying to get them as close as possible to the surface without disturbing the water.

"Not my story to tell, vixen." He tilted my chin up. "He's a moody bastard normally, but a lot has happened."

Morgan looked up as the light in Jax's room turned on. He took off under the water again.

After swimming, I rinsed off in the downstairs bathroom and wrapped a towel around myself. Morgan was supposed to have left me a pair of his sweatpants and shirt to change into since my bra and panties were wet and my tank and pants weren't warm enough.

I loved the weather on the central coast of California, but it got chilly at night, especially if a storm had just rolled through.

I opened the bathroom door and found no

clothes. I rolled my eyes in annoyance and went to the living room to grab my pants and shirt, but they weren't where I had left them. I eyed the stairs and decided I would just take some from Blake, who wasn't home.

All the doors upstairs were shut, and when I tried Blake's door, it was locked. I heard music coming from inside and raised my hand to knock, but then decided against it. He was home and just didn't want to be bothered.

I turned to Morgan's door and knocked before turning the knob. Locked. Damn him. I looked down the hall at the two double doors.

Fuck it.

I walked to Jax's door and knocked. No answer came, so I turned the knob and the door opened. I peeked in, seeing him lying on his bed, staring up at the ceiling.

"Jax?" I opened the door further and stepped so I was just inside the door. "I need something to change into."

He didn't respond or even blink. The room was dark besides the glow from the pool lights below. I took another step in. "Jax?"

"Shut the door." His voice was gravelly and made my core stir.

The last thing I needed was to be even more attracted to them. They were assholes and I was walking a fine line by even being at their house.

I shut the door and stayed by it, unsure of what to do since he was still lying on the bed. His face was hidden in shadows, so I couldn't get a good read on him.

"Top right dresser drawer in the closet."

I had no clue where his closet was but figured it was by the bathroom, or maybe even through the bathroom. As I got closer to the glass walls that took up half the wall on that side of the room, I saw the small handle embedded in the wall.

The door was a pocket door and I slid it open, stepping inside the walk-in closet. It was neat and organized by type and in order by color. Light to dark. His shoes were neatly lined up on the floor, not one poking out too far.

Jax was a control freak and it made me smile as I went to the dresser and pulled open the right drawer. Inside were neatly arranged t-shirts. I picked a dark blue one and was tempted to mess up the neatly arranged drawer.

I shut the closet door before dropping the towel and pulling the shirt over my head. Unlike in the movies and all the books I read, I wasn't a twig and Jax wasn't some monster of a man, so it didn't even fall to my knees. Instead, it barely covered my ass and left nothing to the imagination in the front.

I pulled open a few more drawers until I found his basketball shorts and pulled on a pair. I pulled the inner drawstring and rolled the waistband. I stepped out of the closet, the wet towel draped over my forearm.

"Well, thanks." I got to the door and stared at the doorknob before turning toward Jax. "Why do you hate me so much?"

I walked to the bed and looked down at him. He turned his head away from me, but not before I saw the tears on his cheeks. I wasn't prepared to see him crying.

"Get out." His words lacked any authority and my heart clenched in my chest for some unknown reason.

I dropped the towel and climbed onto the bed, lying down next to him. He rolled back onto his back again.

"Answer my question first." I put my hand under my cheek on his pillow and waited.

He rolled to face me, wiping his hand across his cheeks. "I don't hate you."

"Yes, you do. You look at me like you want to throw me off your cliff."

He put his hand on my cheek. "You're a job. We're supposed to be getting to your father through any means possible. The shit we've done to you is child's play compared to what we should be doing."

"A job?" I searched his eyes. "Like the mafia?"

"We're nothing like the mafia. Consider us... military. High school is part of our training, and since you happen to be there..."

"But why use me to get to him?" I put my hand over his, the need to touch him undeniably strong. "I'm nothing to my father."

"There's other motivation." He shut his eyes. "My sister is dying."

Tears instantly welled up in my eyes and I scooted closer to him. "Jax..." I don't know why I felt my heart breaking for him, but it pained me to see him hurt.

"She was trying to help a pod of dolphins that were surrounded by the oil." His eyes opened and anger flashed through them. "She is young and stupid. Just because it didn't look like there was oil in the water she was in, didn't mean there wasn't any there. It got into her lungs."

He wrapped his arms around me, pulling me

against him. My hands went to his bare chest and I laid my cheek against his skin. "I'm sorry."

"It's not your fault." His hand moved to my lower back and settled under my shirt, causing warmth to spread through my body. "Every time I see you..."

"You think of her." I traced a small scar on his chest and wondered how he'd gotten it. "If I knew where my father was, I would tell you."

"I know." He ran a finger along the waistband of the shorts. "My father is out for blood. If he thinks we aren't doing what we need to, he will get more involved."

"I might share blood with my dad, but he lost his right to call me his daughter a long time ago." I went to sit up, but Jax kept his arms locked around me. "What are you doing?"

"Stay." He slid a leg between mine and my body went rigid and tingly all at once.

"I'm a virgin." The second it left my lips, I wanted to smack myself. Just because he was holding me and caressing my skin did not mean he was making a move. He loathed me.

"Figured as much." He laughed lightly and his hands went to my hair, his fingers sweeping against my scalp. "I can't deny the attraction I feel toward you, virgin or not."

I melted against him as his fingers worked through my damp hair. "What if it's all part of me being a siren hybrid creature thing?"

He laughed. "It doesn't matter. Are you planning on luring me to your lair to feast on my flesh?"

I gasped as his hands moved down my back and slid into the shorts, his hands settling on the bare skin of my ass. My skin felt like it was on fire.

"You feel it too, don't you?" His lips slid across my jaw and I groaned as he gently dug his fingers into my flesh. "You feel the pull toward us even though you don't want to."

I shut my eyes as his lips trailed to my neck. "I shouldn't because you are all assholes and bullies."

"You should." His hands left the shorts and my body shivered at the loss of contact. "You're mine."

It sounded so possessive and animalistic coming from his lips, but it sent a tingling sensation to my clit. I squeezed my legs around him, trying to squeeze away the ache that had started between my legs.

It was a mistake coming into his room in only a towel. I knew that, yet I did it anyway. I might have changed into clothes, but it didn't change the fact that subconsciously my body had driven me to his door, hoping he'd want me.

He pushed me back on the covers and hovered over me. "Tell me no."

I stared into his darkened blue eyes. I brought a hand to his cheek and ran my thumb over the skin under his eye. He looked tired and worried, but also looked like he was ready to pounce.

"I don't want to tell you no, even though I should."

He groaned and dropped his hips, his erection resting against my center. "I want to fuck you so bad." He moved his hips and hit right against my clit. "But not tonight."

I opened my mouth to protest, but he silenced me with his lips, his tongue sweeping against mine. I moaned into his mouth and raked my fingernails down his bare back. His muscles flexed against my hands.

He kissed along my jaw to my ear. "Let me touch you."

"Only a little."

He smiled against the sensitive skin of my neck and gripped my hip before sliding his hand up my stomach to rest underneath my breast.

"Your skin is so soft. I love how it feels against my hand."

I whimpered at his words, already feeling intoxicated by him.

His thumb moved under my breast and I arched into him, wanting him to touch me higher. I whimpered when he touched everywhere except my nipples.

"Jax, please." I'd imagined what it would feel like to have a man touch me as I pleasured myself. Doing it myself was nothing like having someone's fingers traveling across my skin.

"Tell me what you want, baby. I want to hear it." His hand moved up to rest on my breastbone and I pushed my head back into the pillow in frustration.

My face heated as his dark gaze searched my face, waiting for a response. He knew what I wanted; why wouldn't he just do it?

His other hand came to my lips and he probed at them, sticking two fingers in. "Suck."

My eyes widened a bit, but then I closed my lips around them and sucked. He groaned and moved against me. My hardened nipples rubbed against the fabric of the shirt.

I moved my hand under my shirt and took his

hand, moving it to my breast. His eyes closed as I moved my fingers over his to pinch the hard point of my nipple.

"Fuck, Riley." He removed his fingers and lowered his mouth to my other nipple, sucking it through the shirt.

I gasped. "Oh, yes." I wanted him to rip the shirt off and remove the barrier between us, but it was too fast.

I moved his hand down my stomach to the waistband of the shorts and sucked in a sharp breath as I lifted his hand and moved it between my legs. "Touch me."

I let go of his hand and he cupped me through the smooth material of the shorts. He buried his face in my neck as he slid a finger along the slit, pressing the fabric between my folds.

The sensations coursing through my body were unlike anything I'd ever felt, even when using my vibrator. I was half tempted to say fuck it, take me, but knew I'd regret it if I let my body rule my brain too much. I was already making a questionable decision letting him touch me so intimately.

I rubbed his erection through his pants as he increased the pressure between my legs. The shorts were slick with my arousal and my clit throbbed every time his hand pressed into me.

My fingers roamed across his pecs, sweeping across his nipples. He moaned into my neck and moved his hand faster as my hands slid down across the contours of his abs and to his pants.

I moved my palm across his hard length. I didn't know what I was doing but thought back to what he did to himself in the shower and stroked him from root to tip.

His lips covered mine again in a brutal kiss and he rolled completely on top of me, settling between my legs. He began moving against me like there was no clothing between us.

"Jax... please, I need-" A groan left me as he ground his erection against me and hit my clit just right. "Oh my God."

"Can you imagine me sliding into you?" He kissed along my jaw to my ear. "I bet you're so tight."

"Yes." I moved my hips up to meet his thrusts and gripped the sheets. "So good."

He was breathing hard against my neck and rolling his hips in a way that made me want to spread my legs wider, take off the shorts, and welcome him home.

But we needed to go slow. *I* needed to go slow. There was no telling how he'd feel about this later, and I didn't know if I could handle giving him that part of me only to have him ignore me later.

I cried out as my orgasm spread through my core and my clit exploded with sensations. My body shook and my legs locked as Jax didn't let up.

He groaned in frustration and then was off the bed in an instant, practically running to the bathroom and shutting the door to the small room the toilet was in behind him.

My chest tightened and I shut my eyes. *Fuck.* I should have known I was just being used. Part of me had hoped it wasn't just that. How could someone as smart as I was be so stupid when it came to men?

"Look at me."

My eyes opened and I blinked up at him. His chest was heaving and sweat lined his brow and his chest. His face was softer than I had ever seen it. He looked magnificent.

"Is this where you tell me to get out?" I bit my lip and adjusted my shirt that was riding up.

"This is kind of awkward, isn't it?" He sat down on the edge of the bed and ran his hand over his head several times before gripping the back of his neck. "I don't usually take things slow."

"I'm such an idiot." I covered my face with my hands.

He pulled my hands away from my face. "You enjoyed it, didn't you?"

"I did."

We stared at each other for a few moments before he laid back down next to me. "Maybe we took it a little too far for your first time being touched like that."

"It was perfect."

My eyes grew heavy and I knew it wasn't even close to a decent time to sleep, but I was exhausted.

I drifted off, drowning in the blue of his eyes.

Chapter Twenty-Four

RILEY

I don't know why I expected things to change after what happened between me and Jax. The morning after was awkward, especially with the three of them at breakfast. They had another swim meet midday, so luckily there was an excuse to get out of there.

The next week of school passed quickly. In class, they ignored me, and while I was grateful for the break from them tormenting me, I felt like a used rag just tossed to the side.

Friday rolled around and I was grateful the week was over. The final bell rang and Jax was out the door before I could even ask him to talk. My texts to him had gone unanswered.

I went to my locker to find Aiden standing next to it. His eyes were darting around the area, and when I got closer, he grabbed my hand and pulled me into an empty classroom.

Aiden had been doing what he was told for weeks now. We still talked on the phone and texted, but it wasn't the same as hanging out in person. I missed him and wished he hadn't been thrown in the middle of my problems.

"I overheard them today." He pulled me into a hug and then pulled back, a seriousness to his eyes I hadn't expected. "None of what they said made sense, but something big is going to happen."

"What did they say exactly?" A lump formed in my throat.

"Something about the admiral getting impatient about their lack of progress. Who's the admiral? Like the navy?"

"Jax's father. He wants my father, but I think it's for more than just the oil spill."

Things all of a sudden connected and my knees turned to mush. Aiden caught me and helped me sit down. "What is it, Ri? Should I call for help?"

My mom was with Finn West for years. She had to have known he was different, just like I knew they were different. Is that why she left him in the first place?

Just how dangerous was he?

How dangerous were *they*?

"I think we just need to forget about everything for the weekend and focus on you." He rubbed my back. "I'm coming to your party."

I stood and looked down at him. "You can't."

"I'm done being blackmailed. Let them release the video. Then everyone will see how great I am."

I laughed. "What about your parents?"

"I'll have to deal with them. I can't hide it from them forever. I was just hoping to wait until I went away for college." He handed me my bag that I had dropped. "We have a party to plan because I'm sure Ivy has messed everything up."

I put on a smile, despite my mind screaming warnings at me.

I COULDN'T BELIEVE I was eighteen. Things felt real now. I was on my own and no one cared if I was without a mom and without enough money to pay the electricity bill. My mom probably didn't anticipate it being so difficult for me to get the money out of my trust. If she had, she probably would have gone about it a different way.

Did she just wake up one morning and decide she needed to put things in place in case something happened to her? Did she not think my father would step up and take care of me?

I dressed casually in ripped black skinny jeans and an oversized, off the shoulder cream sweater with a lacy black bralette underneath.

I could already smell the scent of the hamburgers Alex was grilling. My mouth watered as I applied the last of my make-up.

"We're ready!" Ivy walked into the bathroom without knocking and whistled. "Damn, girl."

"Is it okay?" I walked into my room and slid my feet into black and white checked Vans. "I didn't want to wear a dress like you suggested."

"No! It's perfect." She linked arms with me and we headed down the stairs. "Shut your eyes."

I had been banished to my room over an hour ago so they could set up the outdoor area. I really had some of the best friends a girl could ask for.

The night air was cool and I was glad I wore a sweater and not a dress. "Can I open them yet?"

The smile on my face didn't feel forced for the first time in weeks. Guilt welled in my belly but I pushed it away. My mom would want me to enjoy my birthday.

"Open them!"

It was perfect. They had moved the kitchen table out and made one giant table with the patio set. There were candles running the length of the table. Strung along the fence and across the space between the house and the fence were lights that made the area seem like something out of a fairytale.

A table along the side of the house held tins filled with iced drinks, snacks, and a small pile of presents.

"This is perfect." I bit my lip to stop the tears that were threatening to fall.

"Let's get this party started!" Ivy put on some music before pouring Sprite into a cup and adding rum. "A drink for the birthday girl."

I took a sip and couldn't taste the alcohol at all. I'd probably drink too much if I wasn't careful.

As friends arrived, I was tempted to check my phone. I had invited the yearbook staff since we worked so closely all the time. I hoped Ashley didn't show up, but if she did and was a bitch, Ivy said she'd kick her ass to the curb.

We sat down at the table to eat. I glanced down

at my phone. I don't know why I cared, but I had expected them to say happy birthday.

"Stop it." Ivy put another cup in front of me. "They aren't doing a good job of redeeming themselves."

Ivy hadn't said much when I told her about dinner with Morgan and what happened with Jax. I couldn't tell her it was something else that was probably making me want them. She'd think I was crazy.

Aiden stood and made a noise to imitate clinking glasses. I rolled my eyes and took a big gulp of my drink, knowing he was going to embarrass me.

"I know this isn't a wedding, but I feel like turning eighteen requires a speech." He cleared his throat and held his cup in his hand. "Riley, you are the best friend a guy could ask for. If I was into the vag, you'd totally be my woman." Everyone laughed. "Don't ever change, because you are something special."

I sniffled and everyone touched their cups together. He was right, I was special, but change came as we grew and had more experiences. I just hoped the changes I was going through didn't ruin my life.

I'D HAD ALCOHOL BEFORE, but after three cups of Ivy's concoction, I felt great. After we ate, had cake, and opened presents, games were brought out. I was a big fan of intoxicated Cards Against Humanity. My stomach hurt from laughing so hard.

My phone rang and Aiden picked it up off the table. "I'll get it, sweetie. You just keep drinking." His speech was slurred slightly. "Hello, this is Riley's sexy secretary. How can I be of service?"

I practically fell out of the chair, and I would have if Ivy wasn't sitting right next to me. I put my head on her shoulder.

"Oh, bitch, we've been looking everywhere for you!" Aiden stood quickly, sending his chair toppling back.

My brain took a minute to process, but then I jumped up and grabbed the phone from his hand. "Mom?"

I walked into the house and shut the sliding door behind me, shutting out the noise of the party.

"Riley." Her voice was barely audible. "Happy birthday, sweetie."

The alcohol running through me made me

unable to stop the sob that came from my throat. "Mom, where are you?"

There was some shuffling on the other end of her phone and I hoped she wasn't about to hang up. "I'm with your father."

The room felt like it was spinning. I had somehow made it to the living room and gripped onto the back of the couch. "You left me! I have no money! They took my car!"

Anger surged inside me and I wanted to break something. I should have known drinking given my emotional state was a bad idea. I had been on the edge of snapping for weeks, but her being with my father was my tipping point.

"I'm sorry. I didn't have a choice. Did you find my letter?"

I wiped at my eyes and sat on the arm of the couch. "Yes. Are we part siren? Why are you with Dad? When are you coming home?"

I could barely understand my words through my tears and my slurred speech. There was a moment of silence.

"I can't come home. Not yet. Are you safe? Did you get the money from Tran Nguyen?" Her words were rushed, like she was running out of time.

"Anytime I try to get help, they stop it from

happening." I was starting to blubber. "I don't know what to do."

"Sweetie, you need to calm down, I can barely understand you." I repeated myself. "Who is stopping it?"

"They want Dad. They won't stop until I turn him over or whatever. You need to make him come home."

"Riley, who?"

"The Tritons. They know about the knife and about me and-"

"You need to run."

"What?" I jumped up and stumbled, catching myself with a hand on the wall. "Run? Mom, what's going on?"

I heard a door slam on the other end of the phone and my chest hurt from how fast my heart was beating.

"I love you. Run."

The phone went silent and I looked at the ended call on the screen. I tried redialing the number, but all I got was a busy signal.

"Fuck!" I threw my phone on the couch and turned back to the back patio. My friends were laughing and having a good time. I couldn't go out there and ruin their fun.

There was a knock on the door and I wiped my tears before unsteadily walking to it. The last drink I'd had was really starting to catch up with me.

I flung the door open. I should have looked through the peephole.

Chapter Twenty-Five

BLAKE

*S*ometimes there is no choice besides a choice you don't want to make. To defy the admiral would mean imprisonment or worse. Just because Jax was his son didn't mean jack shit.

We parked in front of Riley's house and got out. We could hear laughing from the back as we walked to the front door. We weren't sure how we were going to go about doing what we needed to do, but we were out of time.

"This is really fucked up. It's her birthday." Morgan was ready to take whatever consequence was thrown at him. He had nothing to lose. His family was dead and he had no one besides us. "What if we-"

"No." Jax knocked on the door. "He just wants

to use her to lure her dad and mom in. It will be fine."

We had found out at the beginning of the week that Riley's mom was shacking up with Robert. What kind of mother leaves her child to be with a criminal?

All week Jax's dad had been on us to bring Riley to him so he could send a clear message to Natalia and Robert. All week we had delayed the inevitable. Either we brought her to Admiral West or he'd send others.

We couldn't risk other tritons coming into contact with her. We were still unsure of the power she had over us. We didn't feel like we were being lured in by her, but the pull to be near her was strong.

The door opened and my eyes quickly scanned the room. Everyone was outside.

"Hi." She steadied herself by leaning against the open door. Her eyes were glossy with unshed tears and her lips quirked up. "My birthday wouldn't be complete without you three."

Was that sarcasm or was she serious?

"Are you drunk?" Jax sounded surprised and grabbed my arm to stop me from moving forward.

She laughed and a hiccup came out. "Me? Riley Kline, drunk?"

She pushed off the door, causing it to bounce off the wall and hit her as she moved forward. She stumbled right into Morgan, who had been concerningly quiet since we got the phone call earlier that our time was up.

"Momo, why the mean mug?" She had ahold of his biceps and patted his cheek with her free hand. "Did you know that I let Jax dry hump me last weekend?"

Morgan's eyes cut to Jax and then back to Riley. "He might have mentioned it."

"Tonight, it's your turn." She giggled and Jax clenched his fists at his side.

This was going south fast. I stepped forward and plunged the syringe I'd been holding behind my back into her neck.

She gasped, her hand flying to her neck after I removed the needle. She turned her head and the look she gave me promised pain. She opened her mouth to speak, but the drug that would put her to sleep was already acting fast.

Her knees gave out and Morgan scooped her into his arms and walked toward the SUV without a word.

We hadn't wanted to do this. We had even refused at first, but the alternative was the admiral sending his right-hand men to retrieve Riley.

I opened the back door and climbed in, helping Morgan get Riley situated on the seat as Jax climbed in the driver's seat.

She slept soundly with her head in my lap. I stroked her hair as we rode in silence. There was no coming back from this. She might have been open to us before, but now we had crossed a line.

We drove about twenty minutes up the coast before turning off and heading inland. There was a narrow access road that had three checkpoints with gates to let us through. We came to an open area in the rolling hills and pulled up to the airplane hangar that housed private planes and the land entrance to our underwater city.

The scanner turned green as we rolled through it, signaling that there were no explosives in the vehicle. Jax pulled onto the platform that would lower us into the tunnel.

"No turning back now." Morgan turned around in his seat and looked at Riley. "Are we sure this is what we want to do?"

"We don't have a choice. Would you rather my father sent his top men to retrieve her?" Jax's hands were clenched tight on the steering wheel as we waited to descend into the earth.

"No, but she's never going to forgive us." Morgan sat back in his seat with a huff. "Unlike you jerks, I actually care about her."

"I care about her," Jax and I both said in harmony.

"Everything will be fine." I had been trying to convince myself all week that things would work out in the end.

Involving a human hostage in our world was a risky move from the admiral, but our people were demanding vindication for the damage done to our home and the creatures that lived there.

Robert Kline had built an oil platform east of where our city was. Everything within our power had been done to stop it years ago, but he had deep connections in the government and environmental agencies that were no match for our undercover soldiers.

Jax drove down the two-lane tunnel toward the parking lot. I hated knowing the water was right on the other side of the concrete sides. My skin burned the farther out to sea we got.

The tunnel was a necessary step to ensuring we remained undiscovered. We couldn't have tritons popping out of the ocean all across the world. It was an easy way to access the city undetected.

As soon as we parked, a group of five soldiers came to our vehicle. I tensed and pulled Riley closer to me.

"Fuck." Jax got out and slammed the door. He put himself between the SUV and the men. I wasn't sure what the procedures were for escorting hostages, but it didn't seem too out of place that men would accompany us.

They had words and he pulled out his phone, but one of the men grabbed it from him.

Morgan hit the locks on the door and slid over to the driver's side as Jax lunged for one of the men and was pistol whipped with a taser. He dropped to his knees before he was tasered and fell to the ground. Our bodies didn't handle electrical shocks well. He'd be down for a few hours.

"Get us the fuck out of here!" Panic surged in me and I unbuckled my belt and reached into the pocket on the back seat, pulling out a gun. It would still do some damage with them in bipedal form, but not much.

The tires spun on the concrete. "God damn it!" Morgan pounded his hands on the steering wheel.

He met my eyes in the rearview mirror. "They put up the posts."

The locks popped and the doors were flung open. I pointed my gun at the forehead of the soldier closest to me.

"Drop the gun, kid. You're making this way more complicated than it needs to be."

I didn't know what *this* was, but following Admiral West's order had been a mistake. The men in front of us were some of his top men.

"Blake. Put the gun down." Morgan put his gun down on the floorboard and put his hands in the air.

"Do it, kid. She'll still survive if I shoot her foot."

I put the gun down and they motioned for us to get out of the vehicle. The taser hit me and pain spread through my body as I fell to the ground. My muscles were seizing and my vision narrowed.

We really fucked up.

TO BE CONTINUED...

Made in the USA
Monee, IL
09 June 2023

35521669R00175